HATS, HATS, and MORE HATS!

Written by Jean Stangl
Illustrated by Walt Shelly

Fearon Teachers Aids
Belmont, California

ISBN 0-8224-3602-7

Printed in the United States of America

1. 9 8 7 6 5 4 3 2

CONTENTS

INTRODUCTION

Hats, caps, and other headgear have been worn throughout the world by all kinds of people and for all kinds of reasons.

Over the years, I've discovered that children of all ages enjoy wearing hats and will often eagerly wear one, especially if they have made it, when they are reluctant to wear a costume.

Hats, Hats, and More Hats! provides simple diagrams and directions for making over seventy different hats. Patterns, when necessary, are also included. Youngsters can freely use their own imaginations and creative abilities to transform these basic designs into unique creations.

Hats can provide the motivation for innovative curriculum-related projects. Celebrate holidays and special occasions with a hat, or stage a hat show or parade. A hat is all the costume you need for a skit, one-act play, pantomime, or parent program.

A hat can provide the focal point for study and research assignments relative to history, social studies, art, or creative writing. Plan a hat contest where students create and then vote on the prettiest, ugliest, silliest, or craziest hat. Making and wearing "mood hats" can change the entire atmosphere of your classroom. For example: grumpy hats, happy hats, and hats for the blues.

While making their own hats, younger children will be discovering and exploring concepts dealing with size, color, shape, and texture. They will also be practicing basic skills such as cutting, folding, pasting, and learning to follow directions.

This book provides numerous choices and opportunities for artistic expression and creative experimentation for all ages. Once the basic hats are made, children should be allowed the freedom to decorate them in their own choice of style.

Here are a few suggestions to make your hat-making projects successful. After stapling materials to the hats, some staples may need to be covered with transparent tape, so they won't catch in hair or on clothes. Strengthen punched holes with gummed reinforcements. Some measurements may need to be adjusted to fit different age groups. A pleat made in the back of a paper bag and other paper hats will provide a better fit for very young children.

Young designers will enjoy making and wearing the hats, caps, bonnets, helmets, and other headgear found in this book, so let your kids make hats, hats, and more hats!

Introduction

DECORATIONS

Almost any kind of scraps and odds and ends can be used for decorating these creative hats. Your students may enjoy "brainstorming" decorating possibilities and then take the responsibility for collecting those materials that can be used. Provide clear plastic shoe boxes, large ice cream cartons, take-home style chicken buckets, or other boxes for sorting and storing.

Garage sales, thrift shops, and yarn fabric surplus stores are great sources for decorating materials. Used Christmas bows, ribbons, gift paper, greeting cards, and leftover decorations can be added to your "good junk" box.

Make available felt-tip markers, crayons, and paints, including finger paints and spatter and sponge painting equipment. Collages made from small pieces of paper, crepe-paper twists, art tissue and white liquid glue, dyed eggshells, and metallic paper cut into tile designs can be used to completely cover some hats.

For temporary decorations, young, creative decorators can experiment with fresh flowers, grasses, weeds, leaves, ferns, and even carrot tops!

Tape (transparent, masking, and the colored plastic type), glue, and staplers will be needed for securing decorations to the hat.

The following list could be sent home with your students as suggested contributions for hat decorations:

artificial flowers	Kleenex tissues for making flowers
bark	lace
beads	lids
bells	nuts
bottle caps	pebbles
boxes	pine cones
buttons	pipe cleaners
cellophane	plastic toy animals
colored foil	ribbon
construction-paper scraps	rickrack
cotton balls	rubber bands
crepe paper	sand
doilies	seeds and seed pods
dried leaves	sequins
fabric scraps, including fake furs and other textured fabrics	shells
	stickers
feathers	styrofoam packing pieces
felt	tissue paper
fruits and vegetables	tear-off edges from computer paper
gift wrapping paper	wooden craft sticks
greeting cards	yarn
jewelry	

Hats, Hats, and More Hats! © 1989

SEASONAL HATS

HOLIDAY HEADBANDS

Materials

2" x 24" strip of paper (two 2" x 12" strips of construction paper could be stapled together)

4" x 12" construction paper

glue

scissors

stapler

Procedure

1. Staple the 2"-wide strip to form a headband to fit your head.

2. Fold the 4" x 12" construction paper into fourths (3" x 4"). Trace and cut out one of the holiday patterns on pages 11 or 12 (Fig. A).

3. Unfold the patterns and color them (Fig. B).

4. Glue them to the headband (Fig. C).

HOLIDAY HEADBAND PATTERNS

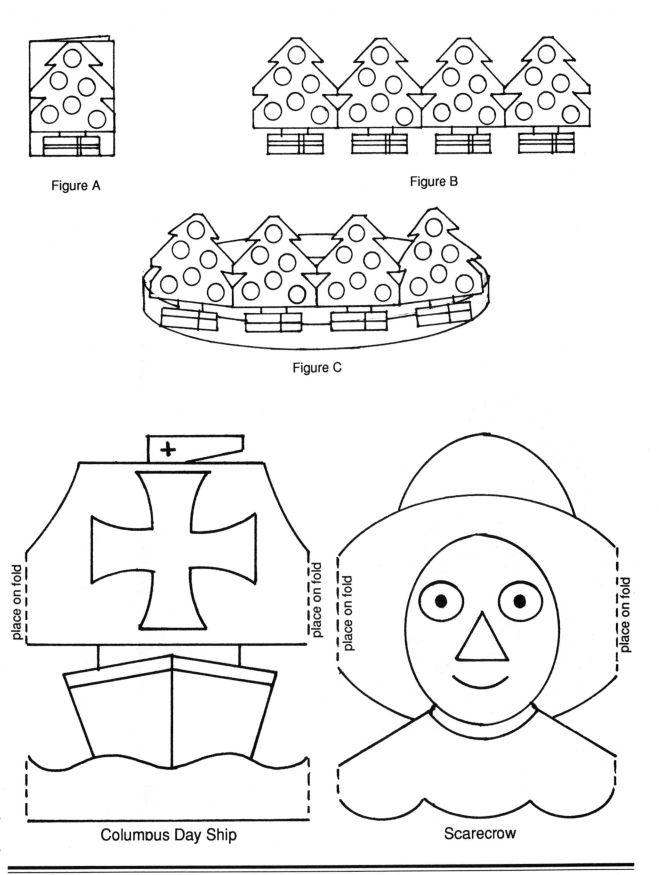

Figure A

Figure B

Figure C

place on fold

place on fold

Columbus Day Ship

place on fold

place on fold

Scarecrow

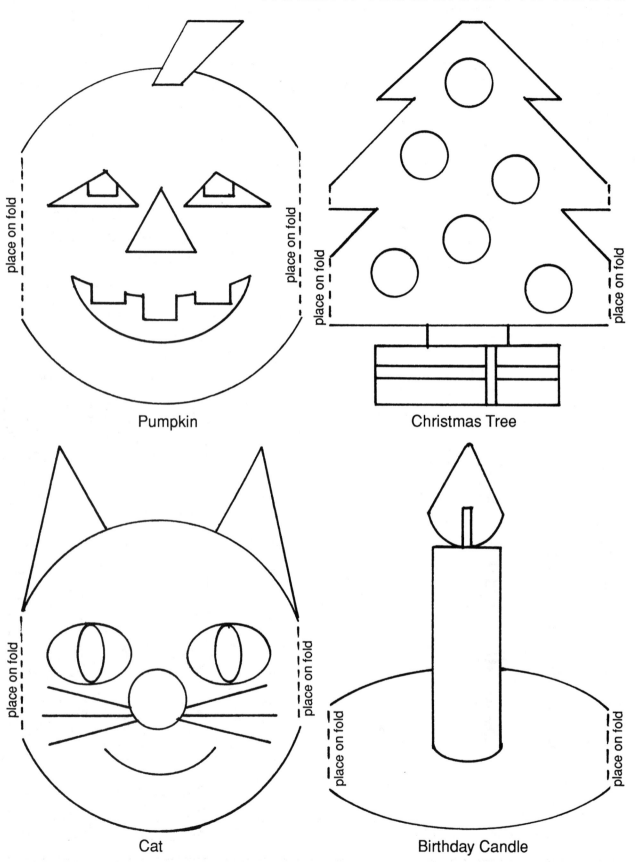

Pumpkin

Christmas Tree

Cat

Birthday Candle

FOOTBALL HELMET

Materials

medium-size paper grocery bag

scissors

hole punch

18" piece of black yarn

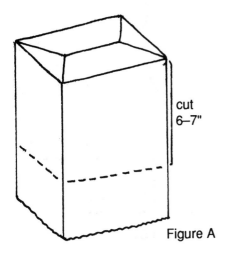

Figure A

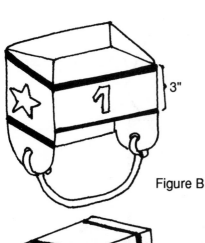

Figure B

Procedure

1. Cut off the top of the bag so that when the bag is on your head it will just cover your ears (Fig. A).

2. Cut out one wide side leaving 3" across the top to fit across your forehead (Fig. B). Round the sides.

3. Punch a hole in the end of each side piece. Tie one end of the piece of yarn in each hole for a loose chin strap.

4. Decorate with a favorite football team's name and mascot or make up an original team name and mascot. Add numbers using the patterns provided.

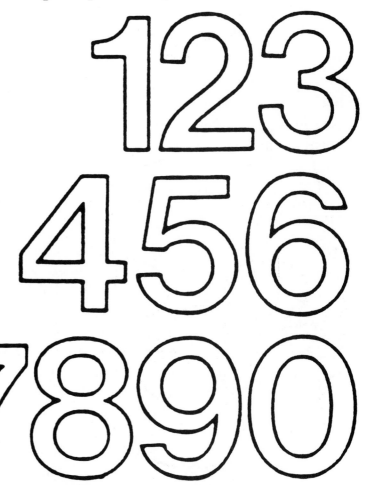

HALLOWEEN HEADBAND

Materials

three 36" strips from a 2"-wide roll of crepe paper (black or orange)

three 12" pipe cleaners (black or orange)

9" x 12" orange construction paper

stapler

tape

scissors

glue

black crayon or marker

Hints for Braiding

Bring the right piece in between the other two pieces. Then bring the left piece between the other two pieces. Repeat again with the right, then left, etc.

Procedure

1. Staple the three strips together at one end.

2. Braid the strips until they are long enough to fit around your head and overlap one inch.

3. Staple ends together. Cut off excess paper.

4. Cover staples with tape.

5. Trace and cut out six pumpkins on orange construction paper.

6. Add face details with black crayon or marker.

7. Glue one pipe cleaner between two pumpkins (Fig. A). Repeat with other two pipe cleaners.

8. Loop pipe cleaners around headband and twist ends together tightly (Fig. B).

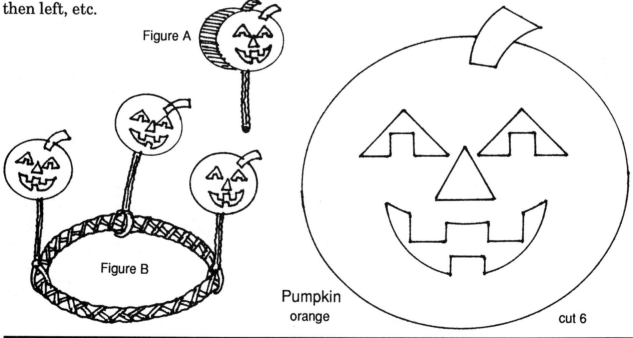

Figure A

Figure B

Pumpkin
orange

cut 6

TURKEY HAT

Materials

12" x 18" sheet of brown construction paper

five brightly colored 3" x 6" strips of construction paper for feathers

stapler

scissors

hole punch

glue

Procedure

1. Cut a 1" strip off the 12" edge of the construction paper (Fig. A).

2. Fold remaining paper in half. Trace and cut out turkey pattern on page 16 (Fig. B). Use hole punch to make an eyehole.

3. Trace and cut out feathers on brightly colored construction-paper strips.

4. Staple 1" band to one side of turkey to extend headband. Fit to your head and staple the other side.

5. Glue feathers to back of headband in a fanned-out position (Fig. C).

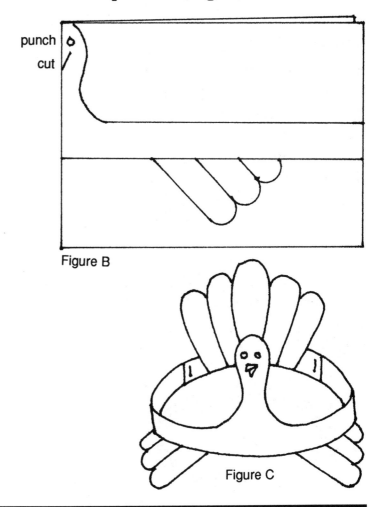

punch

cut

Figure B

Figure C

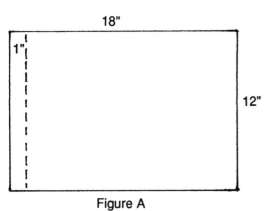

18"

1"

12"

Figure A

TURKEY HAT PATTERNS

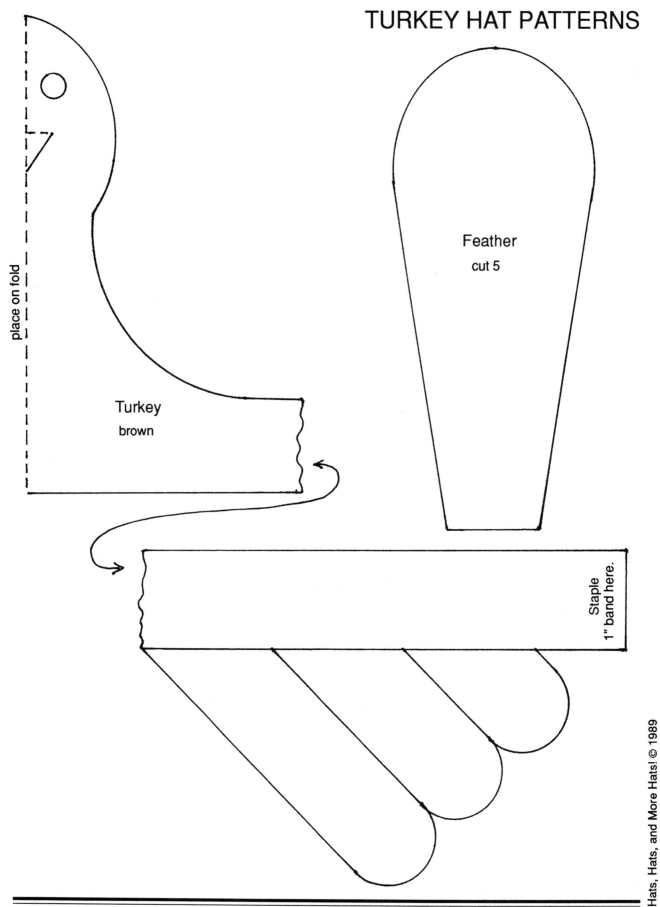

place on fold

Turkey
brown

Feather
cut 5

Staple
1" band here.

Hats, Hats, and More Hats! © 1989

INDIAN FEATHER BAND

Materials

two 4" x 12" yellow construction-paper strips

eight 3" x 8" brightly colored
construction-paper strips for
feathers

scissors

glue

stapler

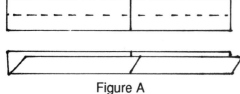

Figure A

Procedure

1. Glue both 4" x 12" strips together to form a long narrow band and fold the band lengthwise (Fig. A).

2. Trace feather pattern on brightly colored construction paper. Cut slits to give a feather effect. Two or three feathers can be cut at once if your scissors are sharp.

3. Glue the feathers between the folded headband (Fig. B).

4. Decorate with hand-drawn designs or additional feathers (Fig. C).

5. Staple the band to fit your head.

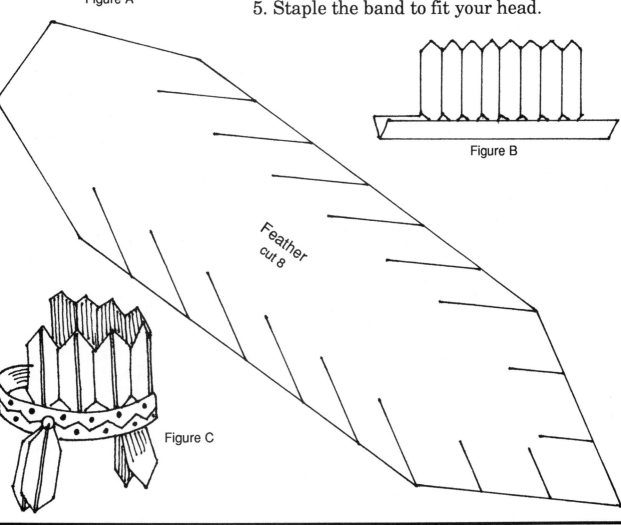

Figure B

Feather
cut 8

Figure C

PILGRIM HAT (boy)

Materials

9" x 12" black construction paper

2" x 12" black construction-paper strip

2" x 8" white construction-paper strip

3" x 3" piece of yellow construction paper

stapler

scissors

glue

Procedure

1. Fold 9" x 12" paper lengthwise. Trace and cut out hat pattern on page 19.

2. Trace and cut out white strip and yellow buckle and glue on hat.

3. Staple the 2" x 12" black strip to one side of the hat. Fit it around your head and staple the other side (Fig. A).

Hats, Hats, and More Hats! © 1989

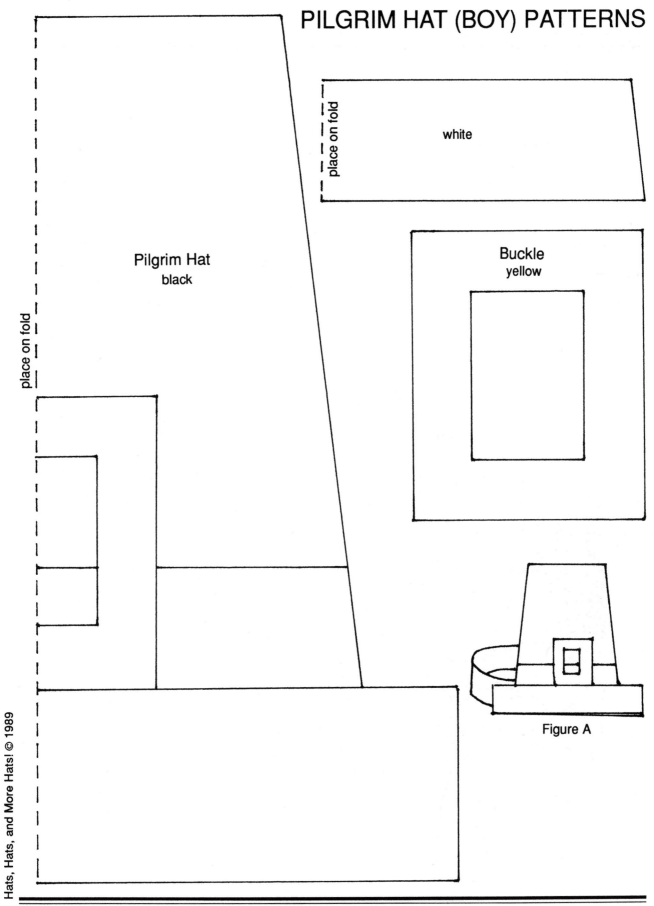

place on fold

white

place on fold

Pilgrim Hat
black

Buckle
yellow

Figure A

PILGRIM HAT (girl)

Materials

medium-size paper grocery bag

scissors

Procedure

1. Fold the bag and lay it flat. Measure 6" from the bottom and mark a cutting line (Fig. A).

2. Cut on the cutting line and cut off one large side (Fig. B).

3. Fold back the front of the bag 2" (Fig. C).

4. Fold the corners of the 2" band forward to make triangular-shaped tabs on the sides of the hat (Fig. D).

5. Decorate.

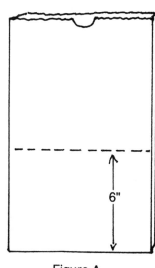

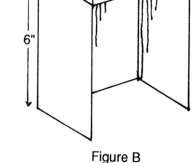

Figure B

6"

Figure A

6"

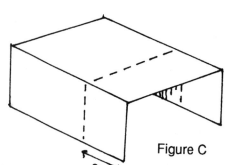

Figure C

2"

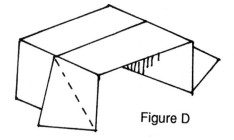

Figure D

Hats, Hats, and More Hats! © 1989

SANTA'S CAP

Materials

18" x 24" red crepe paper

8 cotton balls

glue

stapler

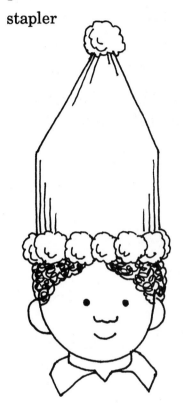

Procedure

1. Make two 1" folds across the 24" edge of the paper (Fig. A).

2. Shape into a cylinder that fits your head and staple at the top and bottom. Glue the seam together between the staples (Fig. B).

3. Flatten the hat with the seam side up. Fold corners A and B in about 1" (Fig. C).

4. Fold edges C and D into the seam (Fig. D).

5. Glue one cotton ball on the top and glue the other seven cotton balls along the band on the front side of the hat (Fig. E).

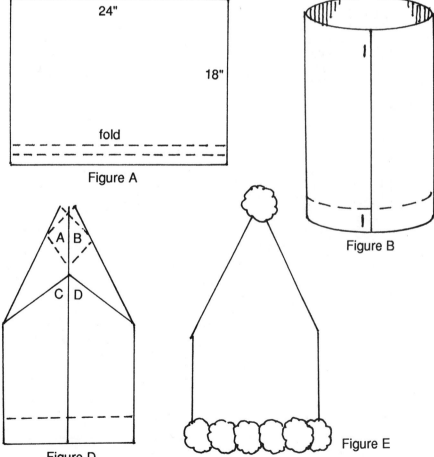

24"

18"

fold

Figure A

Figure B

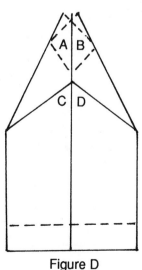

C | D

A | B

Figure C

A | B

C | D

Figure D

Figure E

Hats, Hats, and More Hats! © 1989

STAR OF DAVID HAT

Materials

9" x 12" construction paper

stapler

glue

scissors

glitter

Procedure

1. Trace star and headband patterns on 9" x 12" paper. Also trace a 2"-wide band on the fold (Fig. A). Cut out pieces.

2. Glue the two triangles together to form the Star of David and glue in the center of the band (Fig. B).

3. Decorate with glitter.

4. Staple the 2"-wide strip to one side of the headband. Fit it around your head and staple the other side.

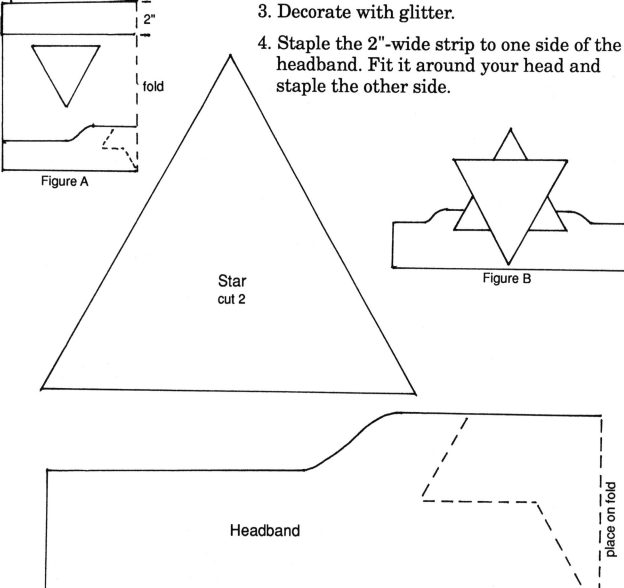

Figure A

2"

fold

Figure B

Star
cut 2

Headband

place on fold

ELF HAT

Materials

16" x 24" green crepe paper

glue

stapler

scissors

12" piece of yarn or string

Procedure

1. Make two 1" folds across the 24" edge to make a band (Fig. A).

2. Fringe the top of the crepe paper (the end without the band) by cutting 3" slits very close together (Fig. B).

3. Shape into a cylinder to fit your head and staple at the bottom. Glue the seam (Fig. C).

4. Gather the top and tie with the 12" string (Fig. D).

Variation

Don't fringe the top. Tie the top with the string and carefully turn inside out to make a beanie.

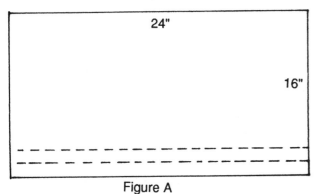

Figure A

Figure B

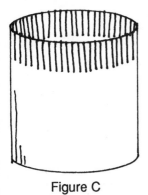

Figure C

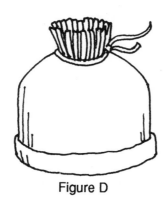

Figure D

REINDEER ANTLERS

Materials

9" x 12" brown construction paper

stapler

scissors

Procedure

1. Cut off a 1 1/2" strip from the 12" end of the brown construction paper (Fig. A).

2. Fold remaining piece of brown construction paper. Trace and cut out antler pattern on page 25.

3. Staple one end of the 1 1/2" x 12" strip to antlers to extend headband. Measure band to fit your head and staple other side (Fig. B).

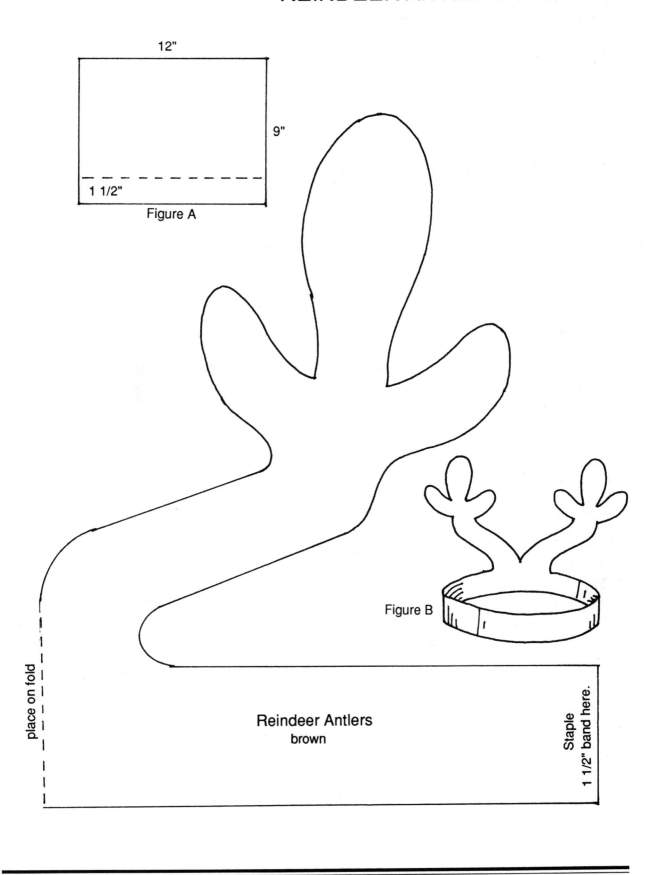

12"

9"

1 1/2"

Figure A

Figure B

place on fold

Reindeer Antlers
brown

Staple
1 1/2" band here.

SNOW CAP

Materials

an old pair of clean men's athletic socks

needle and thread

scissors

permanent markers

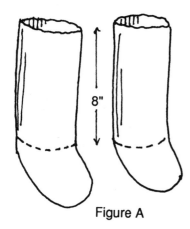

Figure A

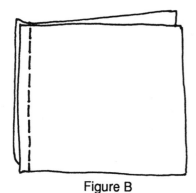

Figure B

Figure C

Procedure

1. Cut the toe sections off both socks, leaving about 8" (Fig. A).

2. Cut up the sides of both socks and open them out flat.

3. Place one sock on top of the other with the right sides together.

4. Stitch the two socks together along one side (Fig. B).

5. Measure the cap to fit your head and stitch up the other side to form a tube.

6. Turn the cap right side out and tie the top together with thread to make a top knot. Roll up the bottom of the cap to make a band (Fig. C).

7. Decorate, using permanent markers. Draw a geometric design, snowflakes, or a snow scene.

NYLON STOCKING CAP

Materials

one nylon stocking

12" piece of yarn

scissors

Procedure

1. Cut the foot end off the stocking so that a 12" piece remains (Fig. A).

2. Gather the cut end together and tie with the 12" piece of yarn about an inch from the end (Fig. B).

3. Decorate as desired.

12"

Figure A

Figure B

VALENTINE HAT

Materials

9" paper plate

3" x 10" red, pink, or white construction-paper strip

two 18" pieces of red ribbon

hole punch

Valentine stickers, glitter, yarn, ribbon (optional)

scissors

Procedure

1. Fold paper plate in half. Trace and cut out large heart pattern on page 29.

2. Fold 3" x 10" strip into fourths (2 1/2" x 3").

3. Trace small heart pattern on folded paper and cut out (Fig. A).

4. Fold pointed end of each heart to make a small tab.

5. Glue the tabs of each heart to the center of the plate (Fig. B).

6. Decorate with Valentine stickers, glitter, yarn, or ribbon if desired.

7. Punch a hole on each side of the plate. Tie a ribbon through each hole. Tie the ribbons under your chin when wearing the hat.

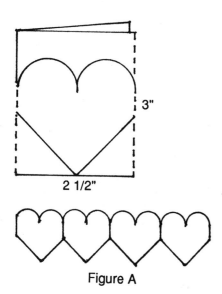

Figure A

Variations

Decorate the top of the hat with various sizes and colors of doilies (Fig. C). Or, invert the lid of a heart-shaped candy box. Staple a ribbon to each side and decorate. (Fig. D).

Figure B

Figure C

Figure D

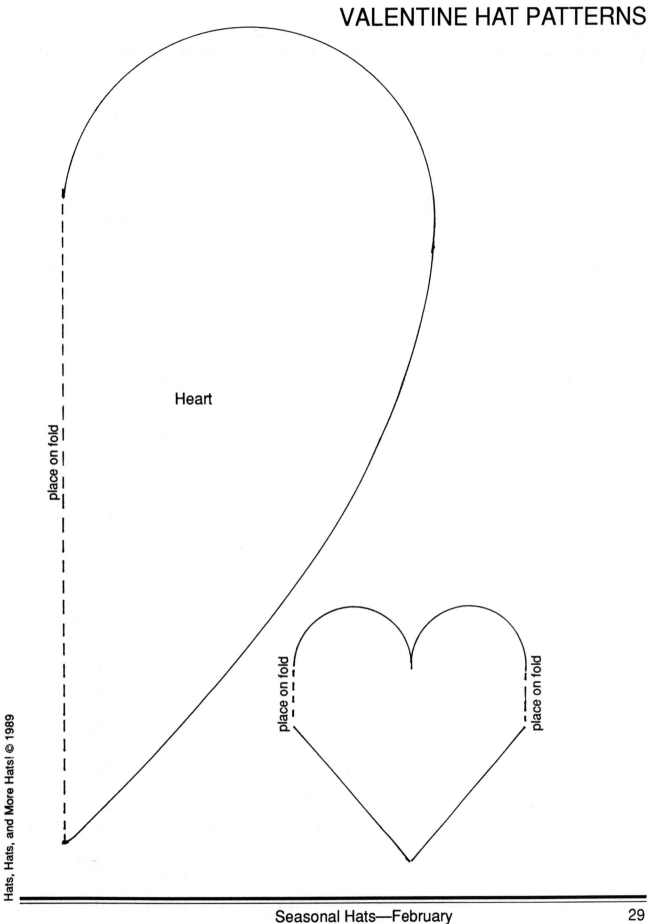

Heart

place on fold

place on fold

place on fold

Hats, Hats, and More Hats! © 1989

GEORGE WASHINGTON'S THREE-CORNERED HAT

Materials

12" x 18" sheet of construction paper

scissors

stapler

Procedure

1. Fold the paper in half lengthwise, and trace and cut out three hat patterns.

2. Staple the three pieces together at the corners and halfway up each side (Fig. A).

3. Decorate as desired.

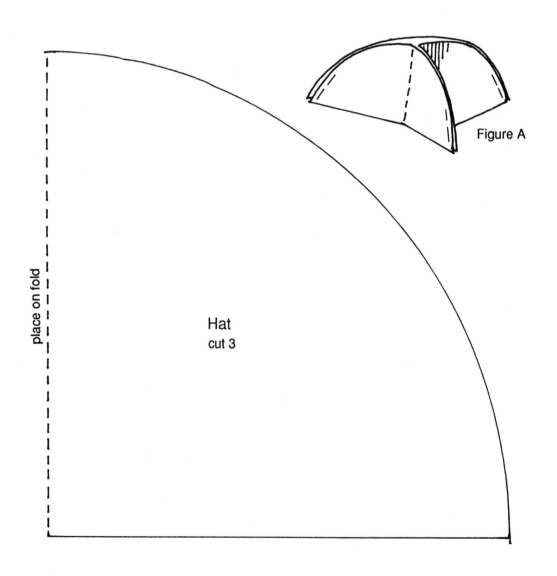

Figure A

place on fold

Hat
cut 3

GEORGE WASHINGTON'S GENERAL HAT

Materials

12" x 18" black construction paper

4" x 4" white construction paper

3" x 3" yellow construction paper

6" blue ribbon

scissors

tape

Procedure

1. Fold 12" x 18" sheet of construction paper into fourths. Trace and cut out hat pattern on page 32.

2. Leave the hat folded in half and cut in 5" on the center fold line (Fig. A). When the hat is opened up, you will have a 10" slit down the center.

3. Carefully try on the hat and lengthen the slit if needed to fit your head. Reinforce the ends of the slit with tape.

4. Trace and cut out medallion and medallion center. Glue the yellow center in place.

5. Cut the 6" ribbon in half and cut each end in an inverted V. Glue both pieces of ribbon to the medallion and glue the medallion on the hat (Fig. B).

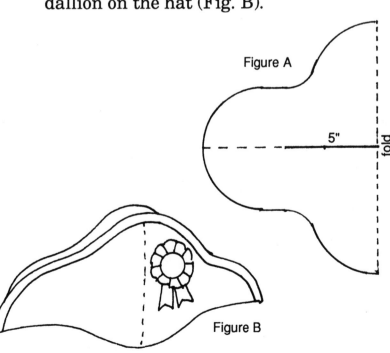

Figure A

5"

fold

Figure B

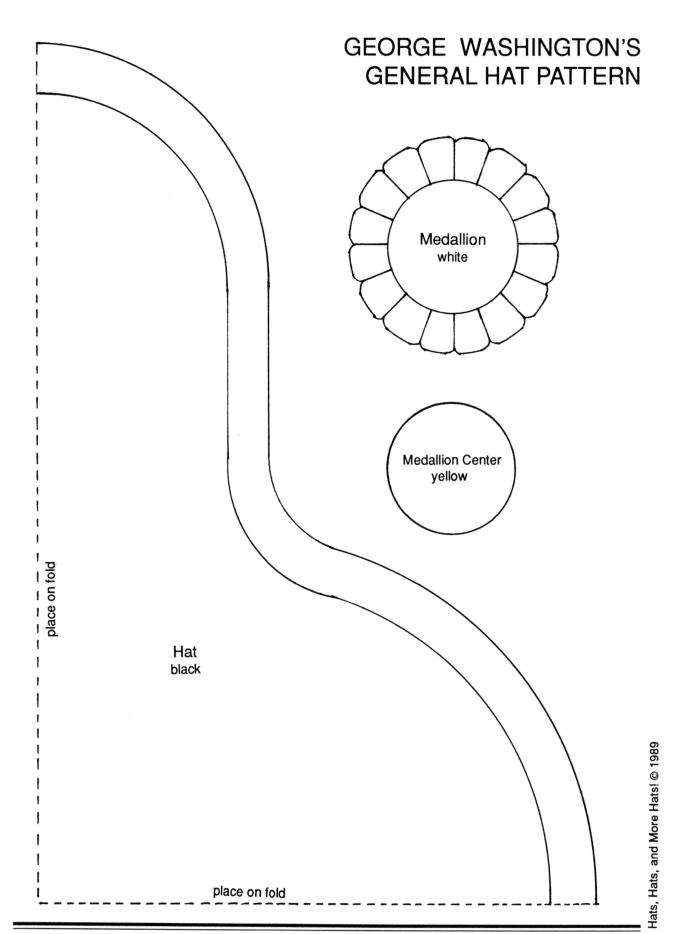

GEORGE WASHINGTON'S GENERAL HAT PATTERN

Medallion
white

Medallion Center
yellow

place on fold

Hat
black

place on fold

Hats, Hats, and More Hats! © 1989

ABRAHAM LINCOLN HAT

Materials

oatmeal box with lid

9" paper plate

black paint and brush

two yards black yarn

glue

pencil

Procedure

1. Glue the bottom of the box to the center of the plate.

2. Punch a hole with your pencil on each side of the plate next to the box.

3. Paint the box and the plate black and allow to dry.

4. Run the yarn up through one hole, over the top of the box, and down through the other hole. Leave enough yarn on each end to tie under your chin (Fig. A).

Figure A

SHAMROCK HAT

Materials

clean cottage-cheese carton or similar carton

two 18" pieces of green yarn

three 6" green pipe cleaners

9" x 12" green construction paper

glue

scissors

hole punch

Procedure

1. Punch two holes on opposite sides of the carton just above the rim. Tie one piece of yarn through each hole (Fig. A).

2. Fold the green construction paper lengthwise and trace three shamrock patterns on the folded paper and cut them out. You will have six shamrocks.

3. Glue each pipe cleaner between two shamrocks (Fig. B).

4. Make three holes in the top of your hat. Put one shamrock stem in each hole. Bend the ends of the stems on the inside of the hat to secure them in place (Fig. C).

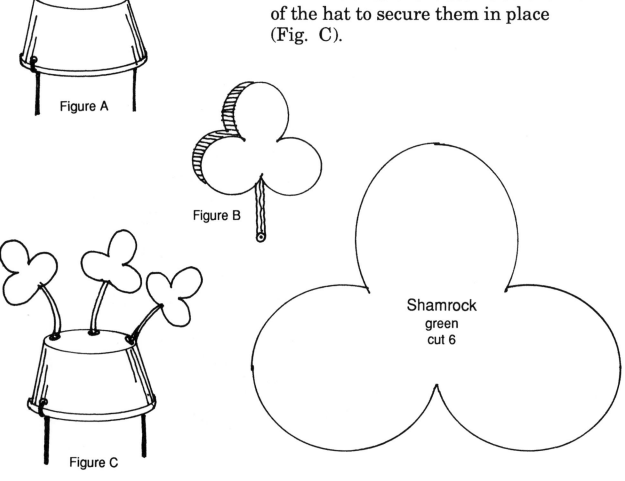

Figure A

Figure B

Figure C

Shamrock
green
cut 6

EASTER BASKET HAT

Materials

plastic berry box

36" of 1/4" wide ribbon

green tissue or crepe paper to make grass strips

Easter Bunny patterns on page 36

scissors

glue

Procedure

1. Weave the ribbon across the bottom of the basket so that the ends extend equally on each side (Fig. A).

2. Cut the crepe or tissue paper into small strips to make grass and put it in the basket.

3. Color and cut out the rabbits.

4. Place the tab of the rabbit over the edge of the basket and glue in place. Repeat on other three sides (Fig. B).

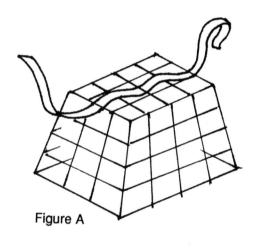

Figure A

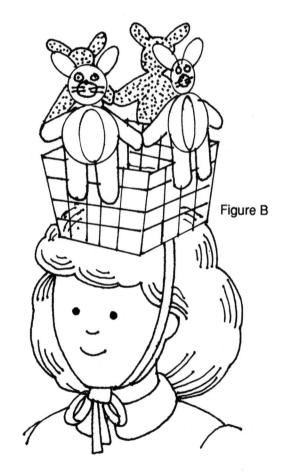

Figure B

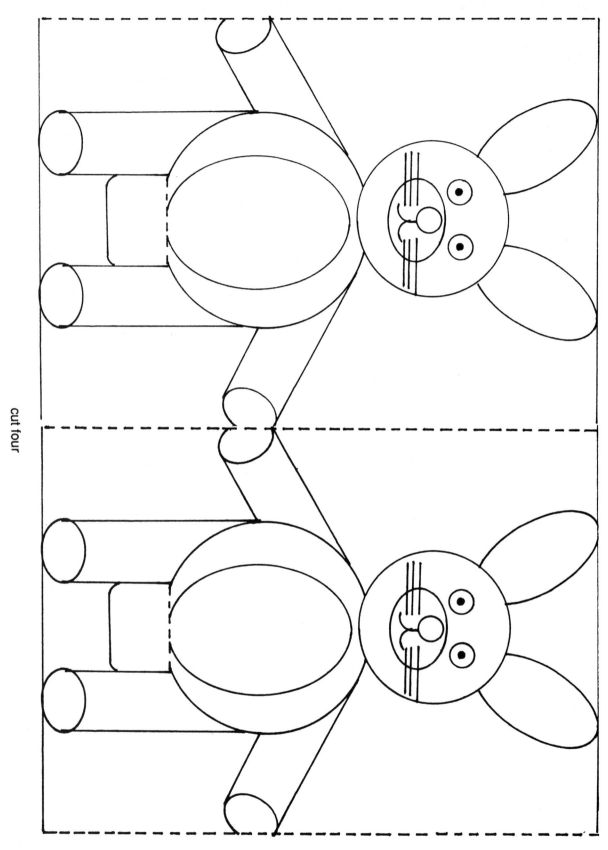

cut four

Hats, Hats, and More Hats! © 1989

EASTER BUNNY BONNET

Materials

9" x 12" purple construction paper

6" x 9" pink construction paper

2" x 3" white construction paper

two 18" pieces of ribbon

stapler

scissors

crayons or markers

glue

Procedure

1. Fold 9" x 12" purple paper in half (6" x 9"). Trace and cut out bonnet pattern on page 38.

2. Staple a ribbon to each corner (Fig. A).

3. Fold 6" x 9" pink paper in half and trace bunny pattern. Cut bunny out.

4. Trace and cut out egg pattern on 2" x 3" white construction paper. Glue egg to unfolded bunnies.

5. Add face details to bunnies and decorate egg with crayons or markers.

6. Fold tabs on bunnies and glue tabs to the front of the bonnet (Fig. B).

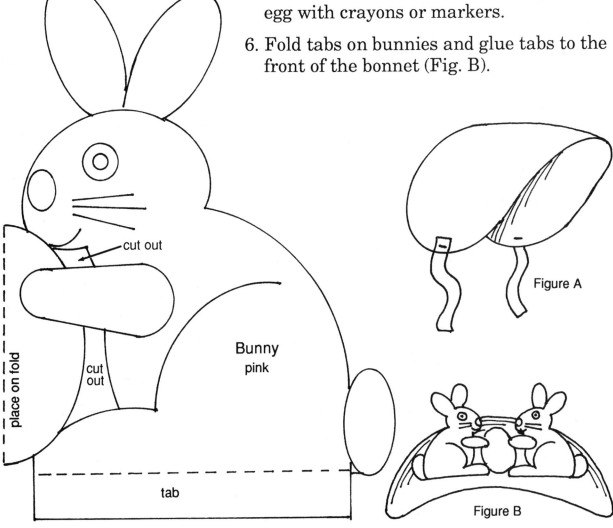

cut out

place on fold

cut out

Bunny
pink

tab

Figure A

Figure B

Hats, Hats, and More Hats! © 1989

EASTER BUNNY BONNET PATTERNS

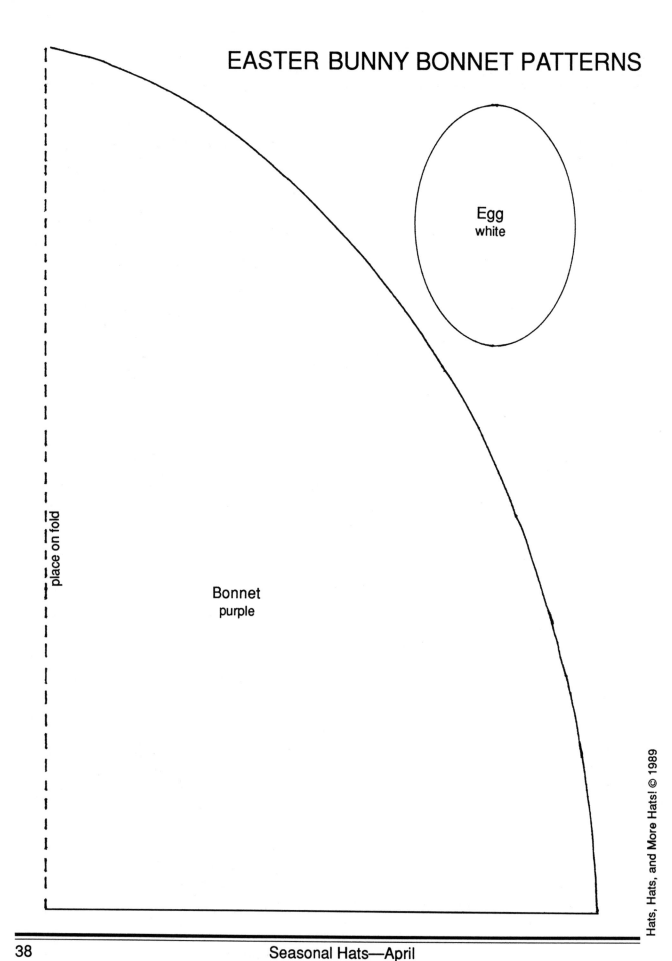

place on fold

Egg
white

Bonnet
purple

SPRING BONNET

Materials

9" paper plate

4" x 6" yellow construction paper

3" x 4" white construction paper

36" piece of ribbon

scissors

crayons or markers

glue

Procedure

1. Fold the paper plate in half and cut a small slit, on the fold at each end of the plate (Fig. A).

2. Unfold the plate and thread the ribbon through the slits leaving the ends free to tie under your chin (Fig. B).

3. Use green crayon or marker to draw grass on the top of the bonnet.

4. Trace and cut out the chick and eggshell patterns.

5. Cover the yellow eggshell with the white one and glue in place.

6. Add details with crayons or markers.

7. Fold the chick on the dotted line to make a tab, and glue the tab to the top of the bonnet (Fig. C).

Variations

Try gluing green Easter grass or coconut that has been dyed green for the grass on the top of the bonnet.

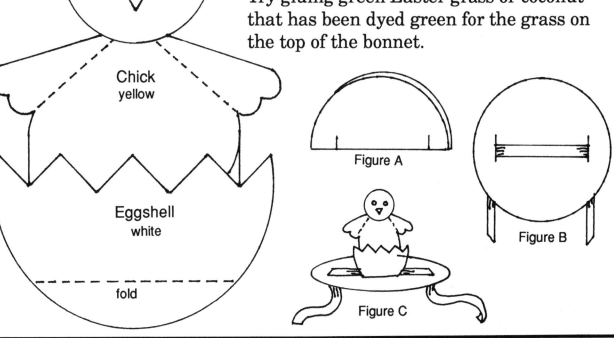

Chick
yellow

Eggshell
white

fold

Figure A

Figure B

Figure C

MAY DAY HAT

Materials

9" paper plate

two 18" pieces of ribbon or yarn

6" x 12" green construction paper

6" x 9" red construction paper

scissors

glue

hole punch

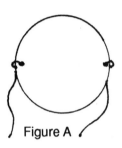

Figure A

Procedure

1. Punch a hole on each side of the paper plate near the edge. Tie a piece of ribbon or yarn through each hole (Fig. A).

2. Fold the 6" x 12" green paper into fourths (3" x 6"). Trace and cut out the flower pattern on the folded paper (Fig. B).

3. Unfold the flowers and crease the bottom of each flower on the dotted line to make a tab.

4. Using the 6" x 9" red paper, trace and cut out four tulips. Glue one red tulip over each green tulip.

5. Place the flowers in a circle on the top of the hat and glue each tab in place (Fig. C).

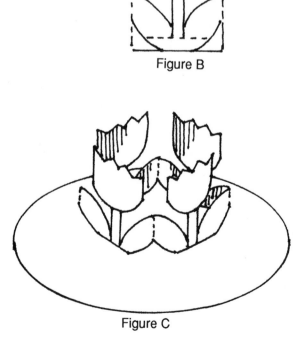

Figure B

Figure C

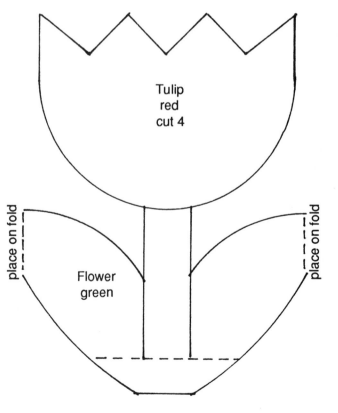

Tulip
red
cut 4

place on fold

place on fold

Flower
green

SUN VISOR

Materials

9" x 12" sheet of construction paper

scissors

glue

stapler

Procedure

1. Cut two 2" x 12" strips off the sheet of construction paper.

2. Staple them together to make a band that fits your head.

3. Trace and cut out visor pattern. Cut slits along inner edge as indicated.

4. Bend tabs up and place visor on headband. Glue tabs to inside of band (Fig. A).

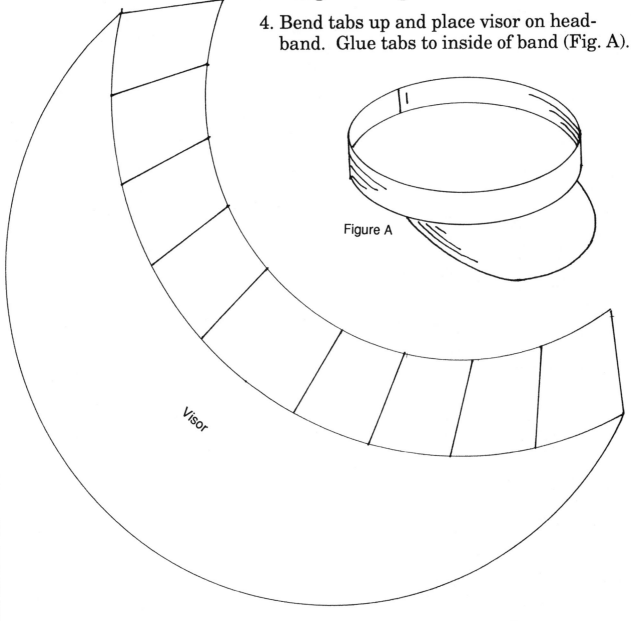

Figure A

Visor

PATRIOTIC-STAR HAT

Materials

9" paper plate

two 18" pieces of red ribbon or yarn

4 1/2" x 12" red construction paper

4 1/2" x 12" white construction paper

blue paint or blue crayon

glue

scissors

hole punch

Procedure

1. Paint the plate blue and allow to dry, or color the plate blue.

2. Trace and cut out three red stars and three white stars.

3. Glue the stars to the plate rim so that they extend over the edge (Fig. A).

4. Punch a hole on each side of the plate near the edge and tie a piece of ribbon or yarn through each hole.

Star
cut 6

Figure A

Hats, Hats, and More Hats! © 1989

HATS FROM
OTHER LANDS

TURBAN

Materials

12" x 18" construction or tissue paper

stapler

Procedure

1. Fold 12" x 18" paper in half (9" x 12"). Place the fold at the top and make a 1" fold across the bottom on both sides (Fig. A).

2. Open the paper up and cut in 2" on each side on the fold line (Fig. B).

3. Fold in each cut corner (Fig. C).

4. Refold the paper in half and staple the sides at the headband to fit your head (Fig. D).

5. Push down the center of the turban to make a dent (Fig. E).

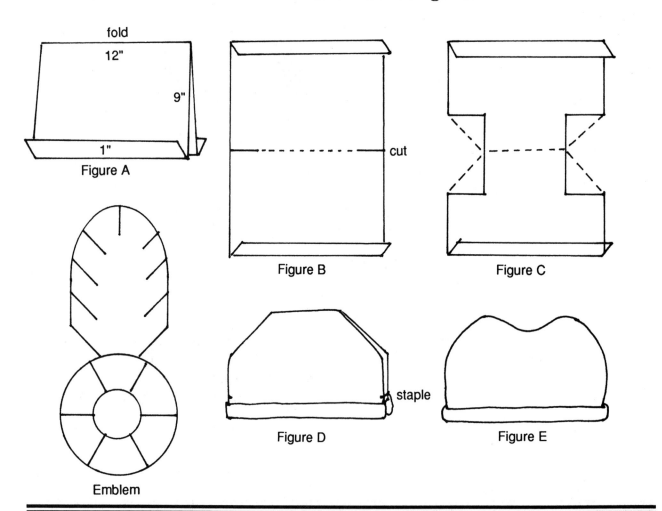

fold

12"

9"

1"

Figure A

cut

Figure B

Figure C

Emblem

staple

Figure D

Figure E

Hats, Hats, and More Hats! © 1989

CHINESE BRAID

Materials

one pair of pantyhose plus one extra leg

needle and thread

12" piece of black ribbon or yarn

scissors

Figure A

Procedure

1. Sew extra leg on pantyhose between other two legs (Fig. A).

2. Braid the three legs together to the end and tie with the black ribbon or yarn.

3. Trim the ends of the legs to make them even and then fringe the ends.

Hints for Braiding:

Bring the right leg in between the other two legs. Then bring the left leg between the other two legs. Repeat again with the right, then left, etc.

Hats, Hats, and More Hats! © 1989

TRADITIONAL CHINESE HAT

Materials

12" circle of construction paper or tagboard

two 18" pieces of yarn

scissors

stapler

hole punch

Procedure

1. Make a cut from the edge to the center of the circle (Fig. A).

2. Overlap about four inches and staple rim edges together.

3. Punch a hole on each side of the hat and tie a piece of yarn through each hole (Fig. B).

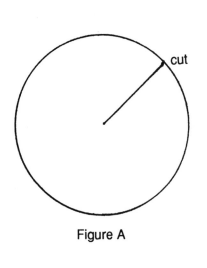

Figure A

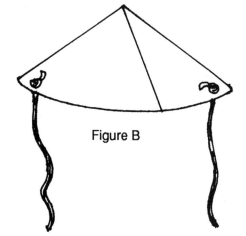

Figure B

Hats, Hats, and More Hats! © 1989

DUTCH-GIRL HAT

Materials

9" x 12" envelope (or larger)

scissors

Procedure

1. Cut the largest possible triangular corner off the envelope (Fig. A).

2. Fold the triangle to find the center and unfold. Fold up both corners to make side wings (Fig. B). Unfold.

3. Open hat and fold "wings" up over both corners so that "wings" are on both sides of the hat (Fig. C).

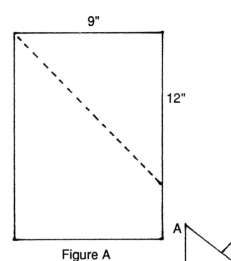

Figure A

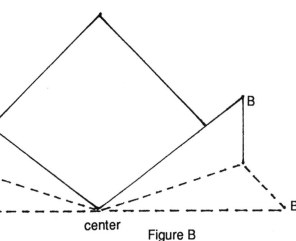

Figure B

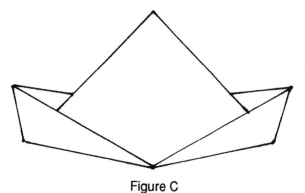

Figure C

FIESTA POM-POM HAT

Materials

9" paper plate

assorted colors of yarn

scissors

hole punch

ruler

Procedure

1. Cut the center from the plate so that the rim fits your head.

2. Punch 8–10 holes evenly spaced around the rim of the plate.

3. Wrap yarn loosely around the ruler 12 times and then slip off the ruler (Fig. A).

4. Slip an 8" piece of yarn through the loops and tie securely. Cut through the loops at the opposite end (Fig. B).

5. Trim and fluff to make a neat pom-pom (Fig. C).

6. Tie pom-poms to holes in rim of hat (Fig. D).

Variation

Glue a paper soup bowl over the hole in the top of the hat (Fig. E).

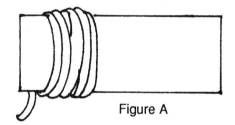

Figure A

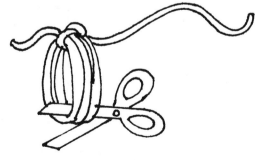

Figure B

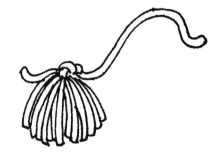

Figure C

FIESTA HAT PATTERN

Figure D

soup bowl

Figure E

SPARTAN HAT

Materials

two 18" butcher paper circles

stapler

Procedure

1. Lay both circles on top of each other and cut away 3/8 of the circle (Fig. A).

2. Staple around the rounded edge about 2" from the edge (Fig. B).

3. Fringe the rounded edge (Fig. C).

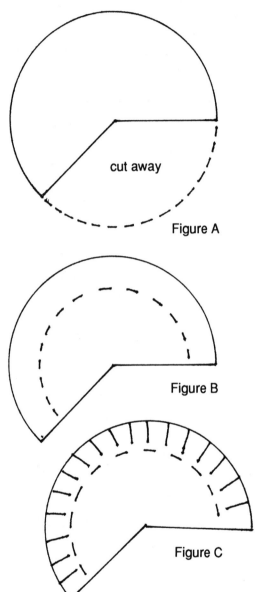

cut away

Figure A

Figure B

Figure C

ANCIENT-EGYPTIAN HAT

Materials

2" x 24" strip of black paper (two 2" x 12" strips of black construction paper could be stapled together)

12" x 18" yellow construction paper

5" pipe cleaner

crayons or markers

scissors

stapler

Procedure

1. Staple the 2"-wide strip to form a head-band to fit your head.

2. Cut 12" x 18" paper in half (9" x 12") and then cut one 9" x 12" sheet in half again (4 1/2" x 12") (Fig. A).

3. Round bottom edges and taper top of each piece of construction paper (Fig. B).

4. Glue large piece of construction paper in the back of the band and glue smaller pieces on each side (Fig. C).

5. Color and cut out both serpent heads. Glue the pipe cleaner between both serpents so that it will be bendable (see page 52).

6. Staple the serpent on the front of the headband and bend it up and forward (Fig. D).

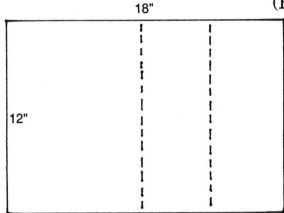

Figure A

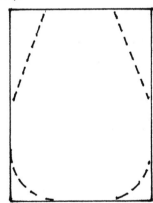
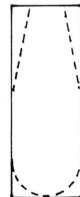

Figure B

Figure C

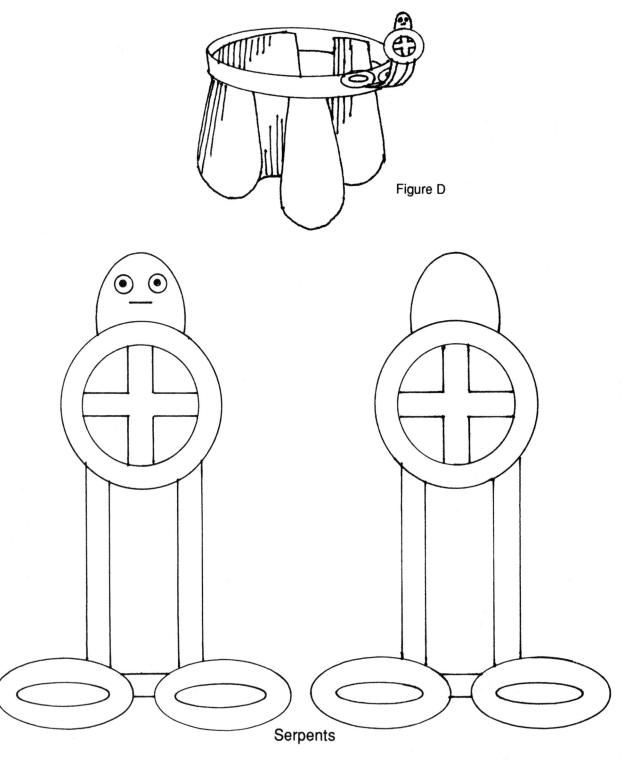

Figure D

Serpents

OCCUPATIONAL HATS

ENGINEER BOX CAP

Materials

cardboard box that fits your head closely

tape

scissors

spray paint

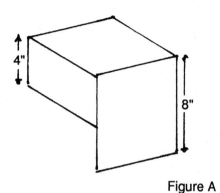

Figure A

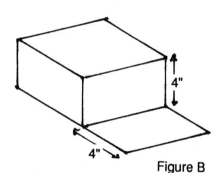

Figure B

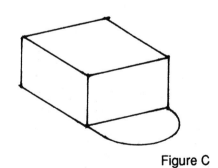

Figure C

Procedure

1. Cut the box down from the open end so that it is 4" high on three sides and 8" high on one side (Fig. A).

2. Spray paint the box and allow it to dry.

3. Fold the 8" side up to form a visor and reinforce the crease with tape (Fig. B).

4. Round the corners of the visor (Fig. C).

5. Decorate as desired.

DRUM-MAJOR HAT

Materials

oatmeal box without lid

12" x 18" sheet of construction paper

18" piece of yarn

stapler

scissors

glue

spray paint (optional)

Procedure

1. Trace and cut out visor and feather band on construction paper using the patterns on page 56. Cut slits as indicated on visor pattern and bend them up to form tabs.

2. Position the visor on the oatmeal box and glue the tabs inside the box (Fig. A).

3. Spray paint the hat and allow it to dry.*

4. Glue feather pattern around hat.

5. Staple yarn to both sides of hat for a chin strap.

* A sheet of construction paper could be cut the appropriate size and glued around the oatmeal box as an alternative to paint.

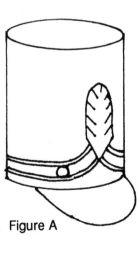

Figure A

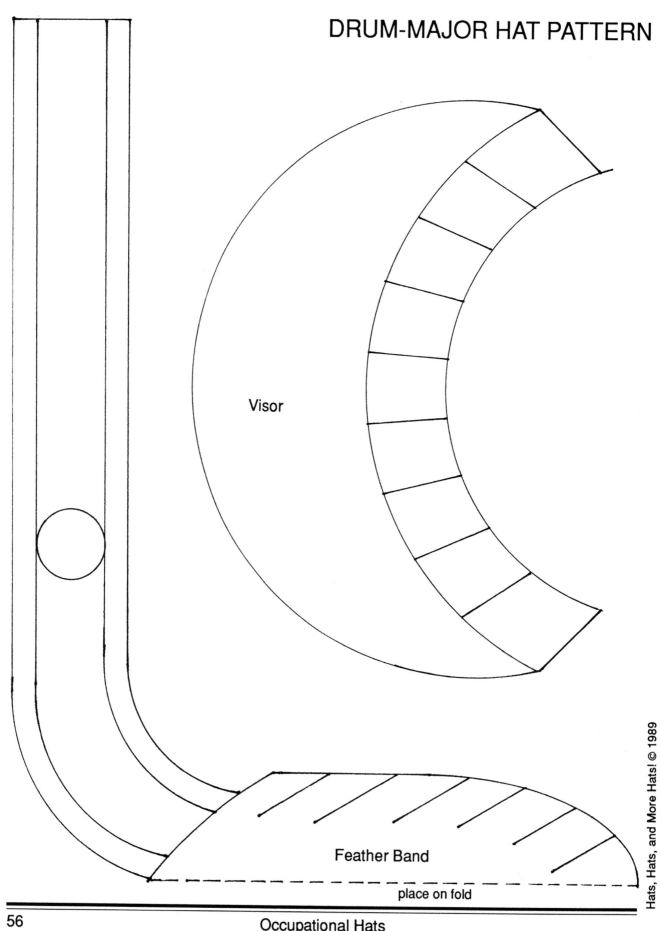

DRUM-MAJOR HAT PATTERN

Visor

Feather Band

place on fold

Hats, Hats, and More Hats! © 1989

SOLDIER HAT

Materials

18" x 18" sheet of newsprint or butcher paper

tape

scissors

glue

crayons or markers

Procedure

1. Fold paper in half to make a triangular shape.

2. Fold point A up to point B about 2" from the top fold of the triangle (Fig. A). Unfold.

3. Fold point C down to point F (Fig. B).

4. Fold point D down to point E (Fig. C).

5. Fold point A over each side (Fig. D).

6. Color, cut out, and glue emblem in place (Fig. E).

7. Feather the top section of flap A and add other details or decorations.

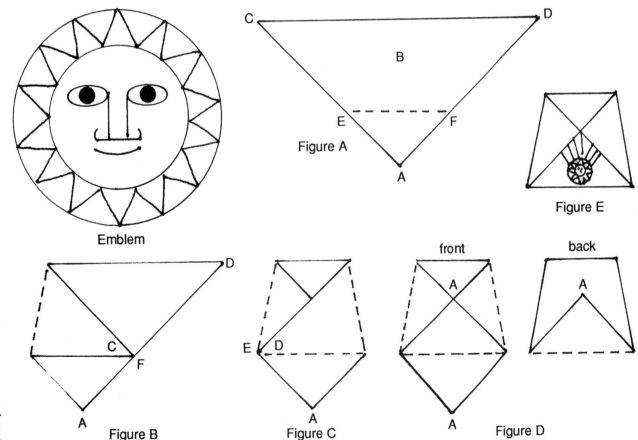

Emblem

Figure A

Figure E

Figure B

Figure C

front back

Figure D

SAILOR HAT

Materials

17" x 20" sheet of newsprint or butcher paper

scissors

crayons or markers

glue

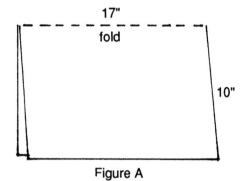

Figure A

Procedure

1. Fold the paper in half to make a 10" x 17" shape with the fold at the top (Fig. A).

2. Crease the paper slightly to find a middle guideline and fold the top corners down to the middle line (Fig. B). Glue the triangles in place.

3. Fold up a single sheet on the bottom to meet the triangles and then fold again over the triangles (Fig. C). Repeat on the other side.

4. Color, cut out, and glue anchor in place on hat and add other decorations as desired.

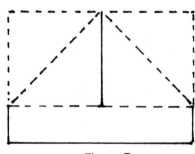

Figure B

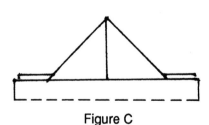

Figure C

Anchor

NURSE CAP

Materials

13" x 24" butcher paper

4" x 4" red construction paper

scissors

stapler

glue

Procedure

1. Fold the paper in half to make a 12" x 13" shape with the fold at the left (Fig. A).

2. Measure in 3" from the left side, 3" from the bottom and draw a cutting line. Cut away shaded portion (Fig. B). Unfold.

3. Fold the bottom 3" band in half (Fig. C).

4. Overlap the ends of the band and staple to fit your head (Fig. D).

5. Pull the center section to the back and staple to the band (Fig. D).

6. Trace and cut out cross pattern on red paper and glue in place on hat.

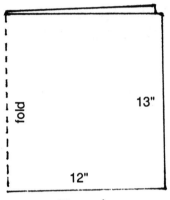

Figure A

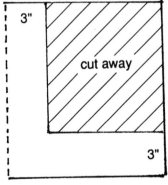

Figure B

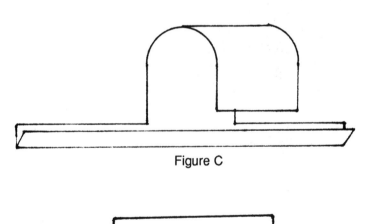

Figure C

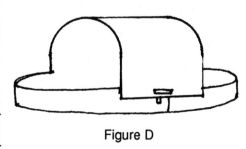

Figure D

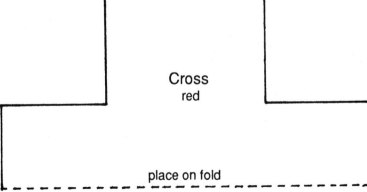

Cross
red

place on fold

DETECTIVE HAT

Materials

medium-size paper grocery bag

12" piece of ribbon or yarn

scissors

hole punch

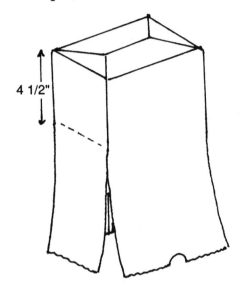

Figure A

Procedure

1. Measure up 4 1/2" from the bottom of the bag. Cut up each side fold line to the measured point (Fig. A).

2. Crease hinges and lay bag out with side sections flat (Fig. B).

3. Measure 5" out from hinge on both wide side sections. Cut and round edges. Leave narrow sides long, and round edges (Fig. C).

4. Punch a hole in each narrow end and bring both sides up over top of hat. Tie with ribbon or yarn (Fig. D).

5. Decorate as desired.

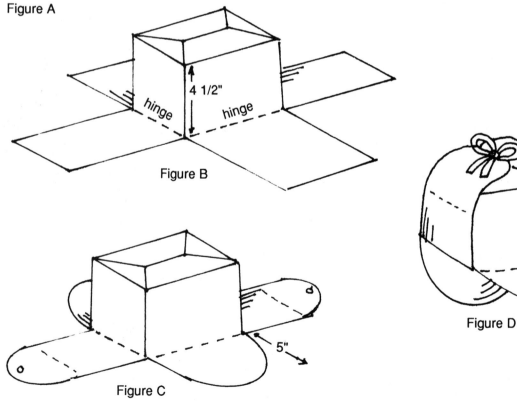

Figure B

Figure C

Figure D

SPACE HELMET

Materials

medium-size paper grocery bag

tape

scissors

crayons or markers

glue

Procedure

1. Cut off the top of the bag, so when the bag is on your head it will just cover your ears (Fig. A).

2. Cut down part way on one end to form a bill. Reinforce with tape (Fig. B).

3. Color, cut out, and glue emblems on side of helmet.

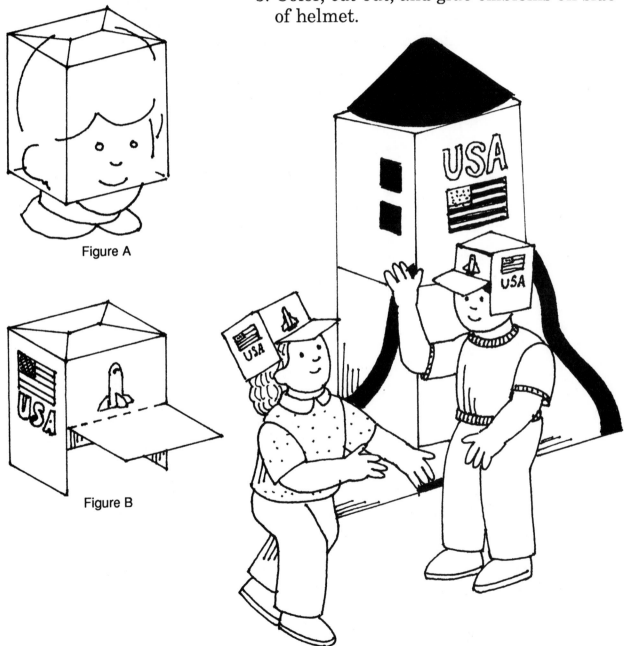

Figure A

Figure B

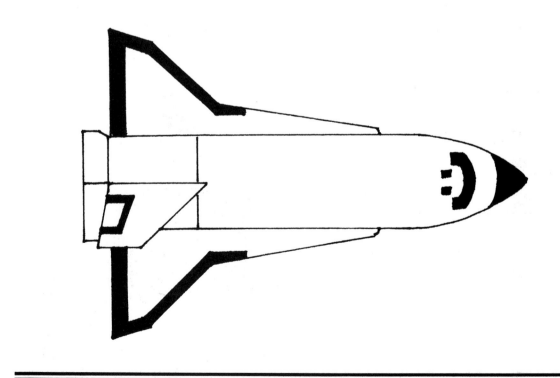

Hats, Hats, and More Hats! © 1989

RED-CROSS HAT

Materials

9" x 12" sheet of construction paper

4" x 4" red construction paper

scissors

stapler

glue

Procedure

1. Fold up 2 1/2" on one 12" side (Fig. A).

2. Overlap the two unfolded corners and staple to fit your head (Fig. B).

3. Trace and cut out cross pattern on red construction paper and glue in place on hat.

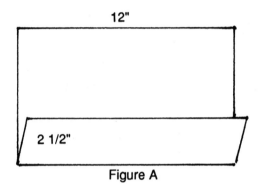

Figure A

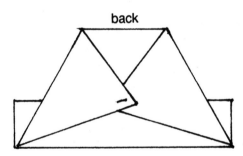

back

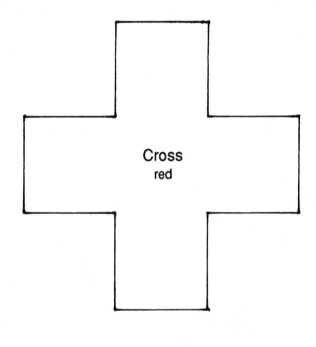

Cross
red

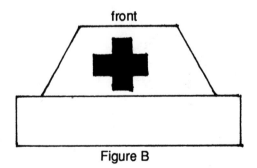

front

Figure B

FIREFIGHTER HAT

Materials

12" x 18" sheet of red construction paper

scissors

crayons or markers

glue

Procedure

1. Fold construction paper into fourths (6" x 9"). Trace and cut out hat pattern on page 65.

2. Leave hat folded in half lengthwise and trace flap pattern (Fig. A) page 66.

3. Cut flap pattern only where indicated by dotted lines.

4. Open hat up and fold flap forward (Fig. B) page 66.

5. Color, cut out, and glue badge in place on flap and add other decorations as desired.

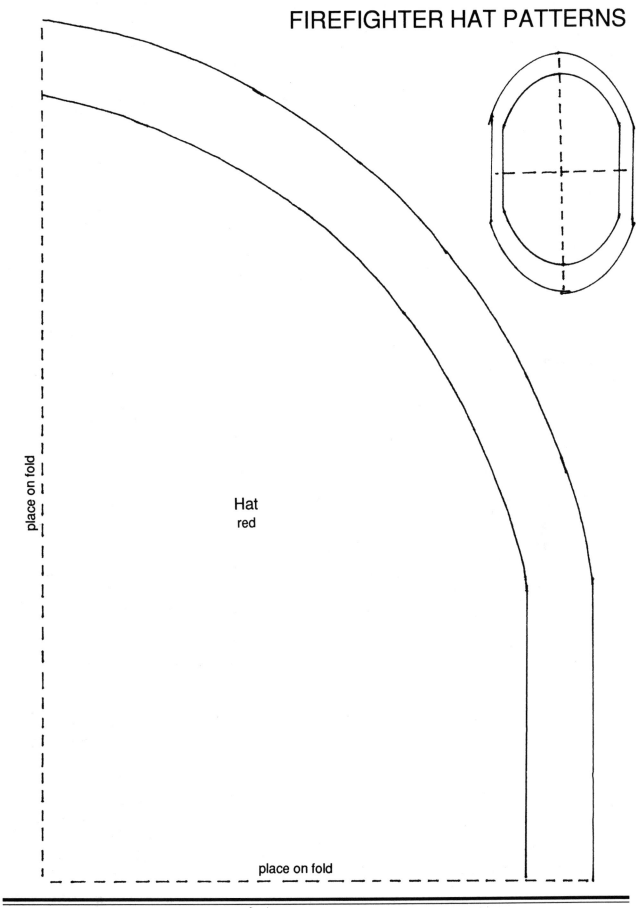

place on fold

Hat
red

place on fold

FIREFIGHTER HAT PATTERNS

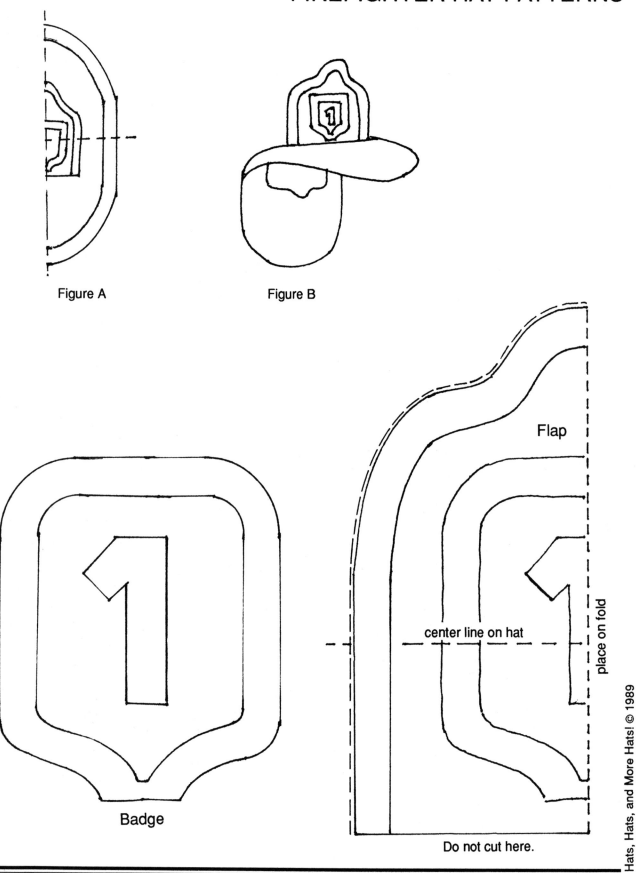

Figure A

Figure B

Badge

Flap

center line on hat

place on fold

Do not cut here.

Hats, Hats, and More Hats! © 1989

JUST FOR FUN HATS

JESTER HAT

Materials

medium-size paper grocery bag

six 6" x 9" pieces of construction paper in various colors

glue

scissors

Procedure

1. Cut off grocery bag, leaving only a 3" edge from the bottom (Fig. A).

2. Cut six colorful triangles and six pom-pom circles, using the pattern on page 69.

3. Fold each triangle on dotted line to make a tab.

4. Turn bag open side up and glue each triangular tab over the edge of the bag (Fig. B).

5. Turn bag over and glue a pom-pom circle to the end of each triangle (Fig. C).

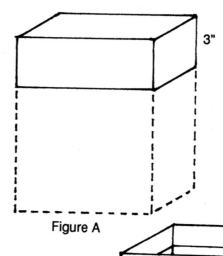

Figure A

Figure B

Figure C

Hats, Hats, and More Hats! © 1989

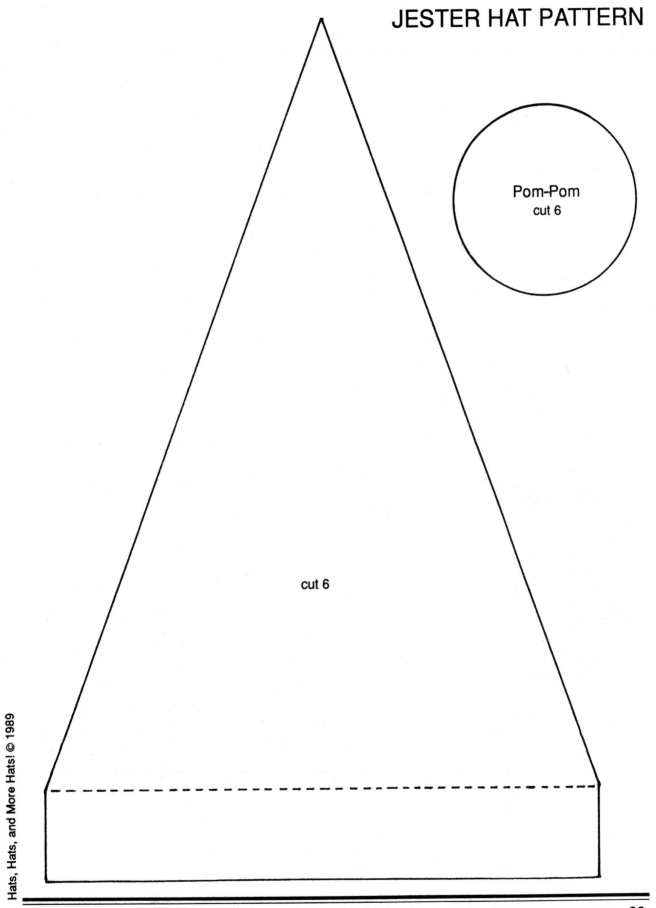

Pom-Pom
cut 6

cut 6

Hats, Hats, and More Hats! © 1989

CRAZY HAT

Materials

one cardboard box lid (shoe box lid, shirt box lid, etc.)

several small empty boxes (toothpaste box, aspirin box, etc.)

two 18" pieces of ribbon or yarn

glue

scissors

Procedure

1. Use the small boxes to construct a box sculpture inside the box lid. Glue boxes in place.

2. Staple a piece of ribbon or yarn to each side of the box lid to use as a chin strap.

3. Decorate as desired.

Hats, Hats, and More Hats! © 1989

WIG HAT

Materials

medium-size paper grocery bag

scissors

pencil

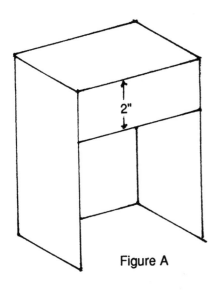

Figure A

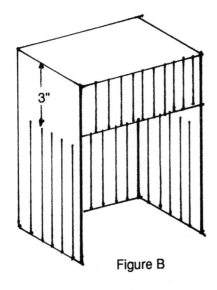

Figure B

Procedure

1. Trim the top of the bag, so that when it is on your head, it does not go below your shoulders.

2. Cut away one of the wide sides, leaving 2" across the top (Fig. A).

3. Cut 1/2" strips up the three long sides of the bag stopping 3" from the end. Cut 1/2" strips up the short side all the way to the fold line for bangs (Fig. B).

4. Roll each strip tightly around a pencil to curl it (Fig. C).

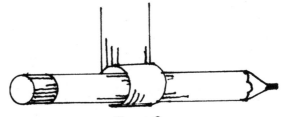

Figure C

CROWN-DESIGN HAT

Materials

medium-size paper grocery bag

scissors

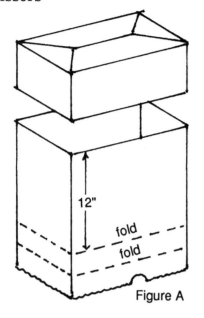

Figure A

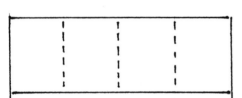

Figure B

Figure C

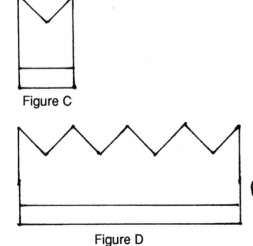

Figure D

Procedure

1. Cut off the bottom of the bag, leaving a 12" tube. Make two 1" folds on one end to make a band (Fig A).

2. Crease the bag, lay it flat, and fold it into fourths (Fig. B).

3. Cut any design on the top of the flattened bag (Fig. C).

4. Open crown and decorate as desired (Fig. D).

5. Use pattern, page 73 if desired.

CROWN PATTERN

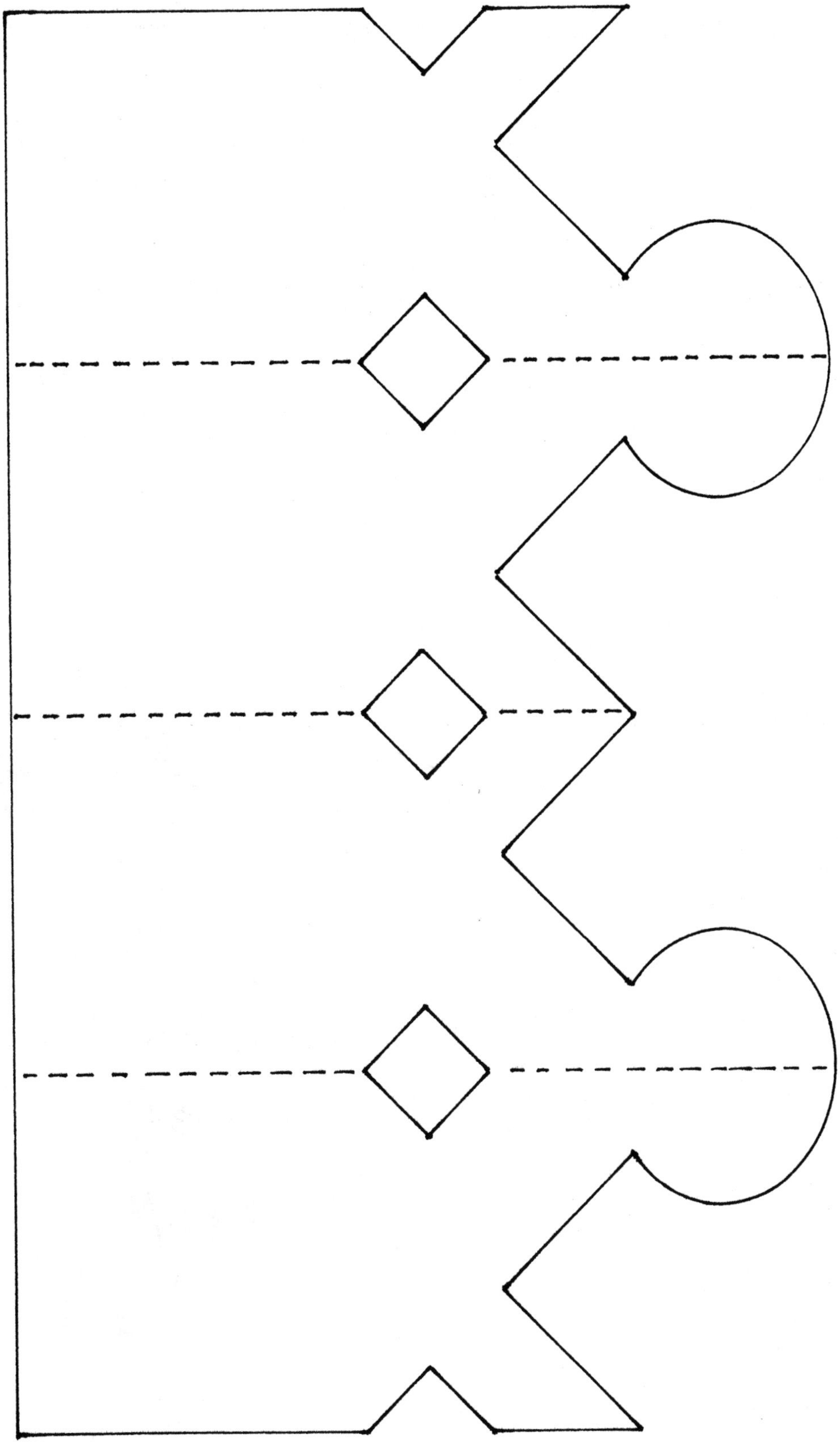

HALO

Materials

two 24" white or yellow pipe cleaners

one 8" white or yellow pipe cleaner

white liquid glue

glitter

water

shallow pan

waxed paper

Procedure

1. Shape each 24" pipe cleaner into a circle to fit your head. Twist the ends and cover with tape.

2. Mix equal portions of water and glue in a shallow pan. Dip all three pipe cleaners in the mixture. Lay them on waxed paper and sprinkle with glitter while they are still wet. Then allow them to dry. The glue mixture will give them an added stiffness.

3. Attach one circle to each end of the 8" pipe cleaner. Twist tightly and wrap with tape (Fig. A).

Variation

Make little sparkly stars and hang them with thread from the top circle (Fig. B).

Figure B

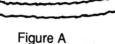

Figure A

Hats, Hats, and More Hats! © 1989

CLOWN HAT

Materials

12" x 18" sheet of construction paper

two 18" pieces of ribbon or yarn

36" piece of yarn

scissors

tape

ruler

stapler

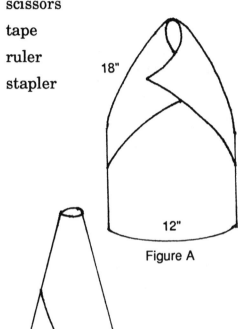

Figure A

Figure B

Figure C

Figure D

Procedure

1. Hold the paper lengthwise and form a cone shape (Fig. A).

2. Tape it together, so it sits nicely on your head. Round the long edges (Fig. B).

3. Cut an 8" piece off the 36" piece of yarn. Wrap the longer piece of yarn around a ruler and slip it off the ruler (Fig. C).

4. Slip the 8" piece of yarn through the loops and tie securely. Cut through the loops at the other end (Fig. D).

5. Trim and fluff to make a neat pom-pom.

6. Staple the pom-pom to the top of the hat (Fig. E).

Variations

Try decorating the pointed hat to look like a wizard's hat (Fig. F). Or, hang a piece of tissue paper out the tip to look like a medieval hat (Fig. G).

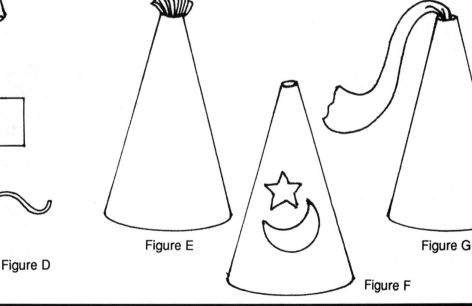

Figure E

Figure F

Figure G

HULA SKIRT HAT

Materials

two 9" x 12" sheets of construction paper

scissors

glue

stapler

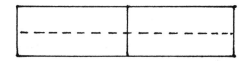

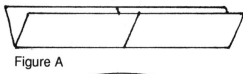

Figure A

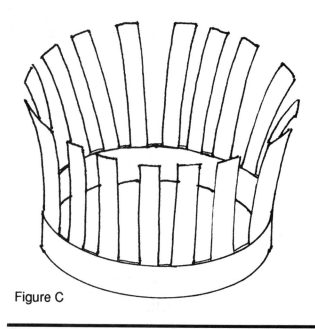

Figure B

Procedure

1. Cut one sheet of paper in half lengthwise and glue both pieces together to form a long band. Fold band lengthwise (Fig. A).

2. Fit the band around your head and staple (Fig. B).

3. Cut the second sheet of paper into twelve 1" x 9" strips. Slip each strip between the folded headband and glue in place (Fig. C).

4. Decorate as desired.

Variations

Paper strips can be curled around a pencil, fringed, or accordion pleated.

Figure C

Hats, Hats, and More Hats! © 1989

SPECIAL OCCASION AND BASIC HATS

GRADUATION HAT

Materials

9" x 9" piece of black construction paper

2" x 24" strip of black construction paper (two 2" x 12" strips can be stapled together)

six 16" pieces of yarn

8" piece of yarn

stapler

white liquid glue

tape

Procedure

1. Fit the 2" x 24" strip of black paper around your head and staple together.

2. Glue the band in the center of the 9" x 9" square (Fig. A).

3. To make the tassel, lay the 16" pieces of yarn side by side and fold them all in half. Use the 8" piece to tie the folded ends together an inch from the fold (Fig. B).

4. Tape the folded end of the tassel to the center of the square. Trim the ends of the tassel evenly (Fig. C).

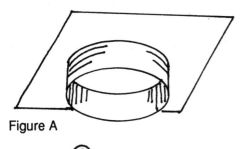

Figure A

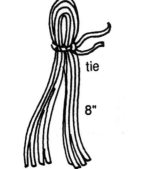

tie

8"

Figure B

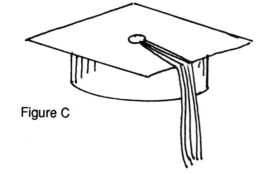

Figure C

PARTY HAT

Materials

14" square of newsprint or butcher paper

tape

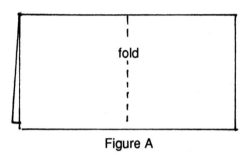

Figure A

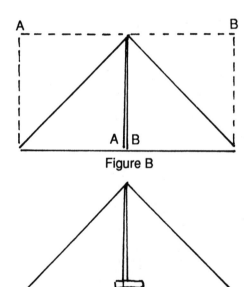

Figure B

Figure C

Procedure

1. Fold paper in half and crease for a middle guideline (Fig. A).

2. Fold down points A and B (Fig. B).

3. Tape in place (Fig. C).

4. Wear the hat with the point at the forehead (Fig. D).

Variation

Fold the point of the hat down and tape in place. Accordion pleat a 4" square of construction paper. Pinch the pleats together at the center and tape to the front of the hat (Fig. E).

Figure D

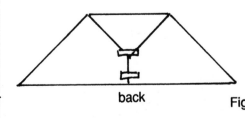

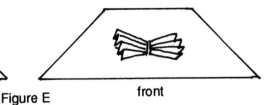

back   Figure E   front

Special Occasion Hats

BRIDAL VEIL

Materials

24" pipe cleaner

18" x 18" sheet of white tissue paper

tape

scissors

Procedure

1. Form a crown from the pipe cleaner to fit your head. Twist the ends together and cover with tape.

2. Pleat or gather the tissue across one edge and tape the pleats to the pipe cleaner (Fig. A).

3. Decorate as desired.

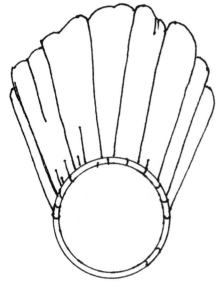

Figure A

HINGED HAT

Materials

9" paper plate

scissors

Procedure

1. Cut out the center of the plate, leaving it attached with a 2" hinge (Fig. A).

2. Bend back the cut piece so that it sits at the back of your head (Fig. B).

3. Decorate as desired.

Figure A

Figure B

BENT-TAB HAT

Materials

9" paper plate

two 18" pieces of ribbon or yarn

stapler

scissors

hole punch

Procedure

1. Make cuts through the rim of the paper plate 1" apart (Fig. A).

2. Bend down every other tab (Fig. B).

3. Punch a hole on each side of the paper plate and tie a piece of ribbon or yarn through each hole.

4. Decorate as desired.

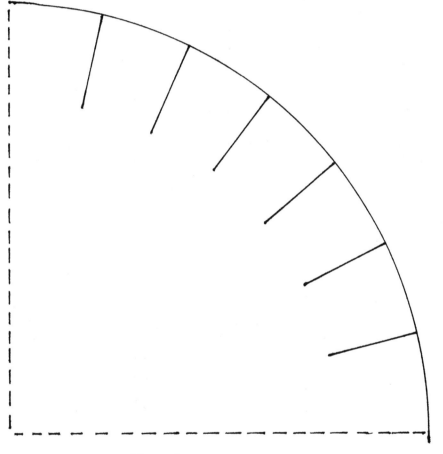

Figure A

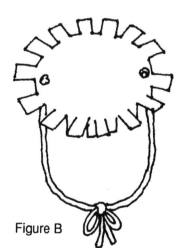

Figure B

CUP AND PLATE HAT

Materials

9" paper plate

styrofoam paper cup

two 18" pieces of ribbon or yarn

glue

scissors

stapler

hole punch

Procedure

1. Glue the rim of the paper cup to the center of the upside-down paper plate (Fig. A).

2. Punch a hole on each side of the paper plate and tie a piece of yarn or ribbon to each side.

3. Decorate as desired.

Variation

Trace and cut out several brightly colored flowers. Fold them on the dotted lines. Stick a green pipe cleaner through the center of two flowers and bend the end to make a little knot to hold it in place (Fig. B). Push pipe cleaners through styrofoam cup on hat.

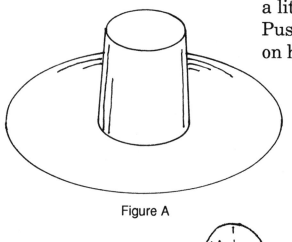

Figure A

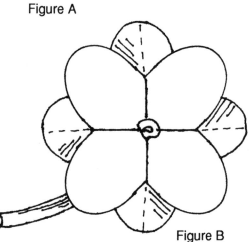

Figure B

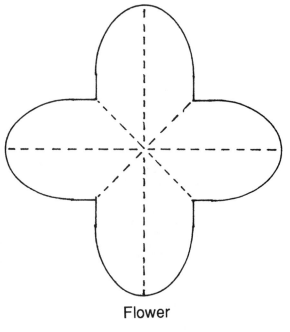

Flower

Paper Plate Basic Hats

FABRIC-COVERED PAPER PLATE HAT

Materials

9" paper plate

two 12" squares of fabric

two 18" pieces of ribbon or yarn

30" of lace

glue

scissors

hole punch

Procedure

1. Glue a square of fabric to each side of the paper plate.

2. Trim the edges even with the plate.

3. Glue the lace around the edge of the plate.

4. Punch a hole on each side of the plate and tie a piece of ribbon or yarn through each hole.

5. Decorate as desired.

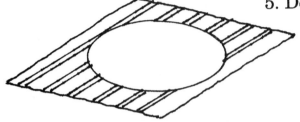

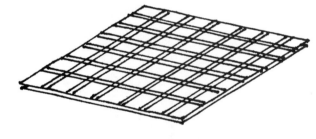

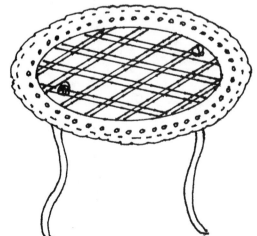

PAPIER MÂCHÉ HAT

Materials

large balloon

flour and water paste

plastic bowl

strips of newspaper

paint

scissors

Procedure

1. Blow up balloon to the approximate size of your head and tie the end.

2. Mix the flour and water in the plastic bowl to form a thick paste.

3. Dip the paper strips into the paste and mold them around the balloon. Cover as much of the ballon as needed for your hat style.

4. Apply three or four layers of paper strips and allow the hat to dry.

5. Pop the balloon, paint, and decorate your hat as desired.

WET-FELT HAT

Materials

unbreakable bowl or pan that fits your head

30" square of felt

24" of fabric ribbon

needle and thread

waxed paper

scissors

large rubber band

Procedure

1. Cover your work area with waxed paper.

2. Thoroughly wet the felt square and place it over the upside down bowl or pan (Fig. A).

3. Press the felt firmly against the top and sides of the bowl or pan.

4. Place the rubber band around the base so that it fits tightly (Fig. A).

5. Press the felt out for a flat brim or shape as desired.

6. When completely dry, replace the rubber band with the ribbon and sew it to the hat.

7. Remove the hat from the mold and trim the brim (Fig. B).

Variations

You can change your hat style by selecting differently shaped molds and by shaping the brim and crown (Figs. C, D, and E).

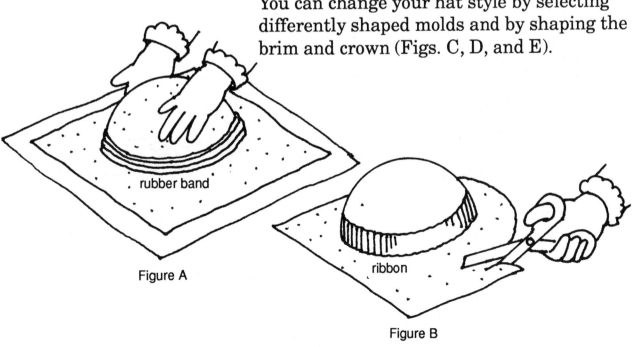

rubber band

Figure A

ribbon

Figure B

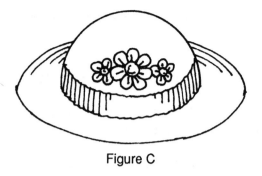

Figure C

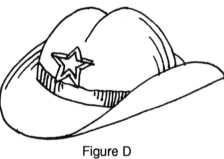

Figure D

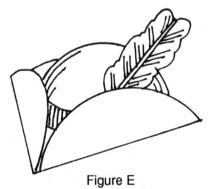

Figure E

BRIMMED HAT

Materials

unbreakable bowl or pan that fits your head

one square yard of nylon net

liquid laundry starch

water

large plastic pan

large rubber band

24" of fabric ribbon

needle and thread

waxed paper

scissors

Procedure

1. Cover your work area with waxed paper.

2. Mix equal parts of liquid starch and water in the large plastic pan.

3. Wet the nylon net in the starch mixture and place it over the bowl or pan (Fig. A).

4. Press the fabric firmly against the top and sides of the bowl or pan.

5. Place the rubber band around the base of the bowl or pan so that it holds the fabric tightly.

6. Smooth the brim out flat and let it dry.

7. When it is dry, replace the rubber band with the ribbon and stitch it to the hat.

8. Remove the hat from the bowl or pan and trim the brim as desired.

Variations

One square yard of lightweight cotton fabric or three full sheets of newsprint can be used in place of the nylon net.

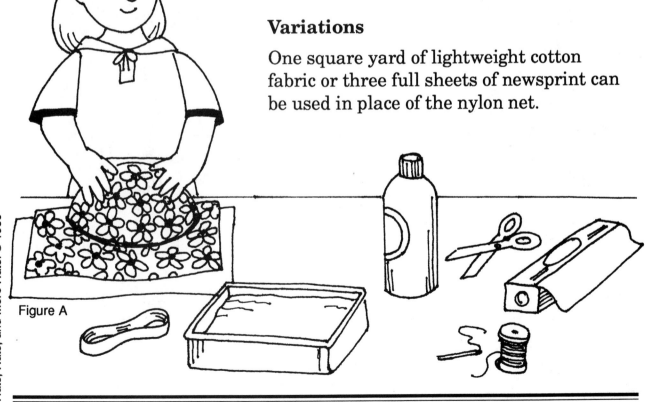

Figure A

ROLLED-BRIM HAT

Materials

medium-size paper grocery bag

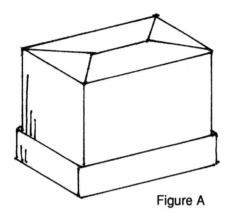

Figure A

Procedure

1. Carefully roll up the bag, forming a brim. Continue rolling until the crown is the desired height (Fig. A).

2. Decorate as desired.

Variation

Stick one hand inside the bag. Push in the corners with the hand on the outside so that the sides bulge out and the top is rounded (Fig. B).

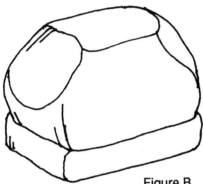

Figure B

BAG BOX HAT

Materials

medium-size paper grocery bag

scissors

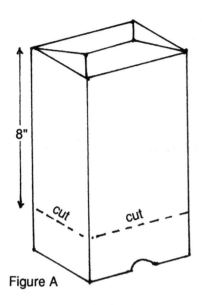

Figure A

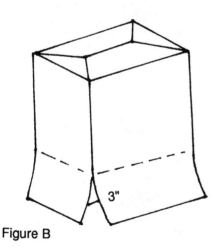

Figure B

Procedure

1. Cut off the top of the bag, leaving 8" from the bottom (Fig. A).

2. Cut up 3" at each side crease (Fig. B).

3. Cut slits about 1" apart on the 3" flaps, and round the edges (Fig. C).

4. Decorate as desired.

Variations

Try cutting points or fringing the ends rather than rounding them (Fig. D).

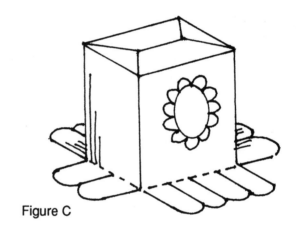

Figure C

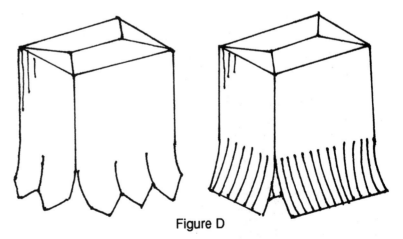

Figure D

ROLLED-BAND HAT

Materials

medium-size paper grocery bag

scissors

stapler

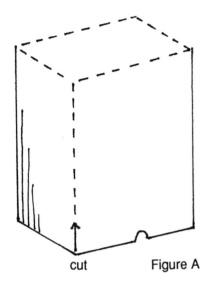

cut   Figure A

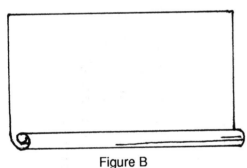

Figure B

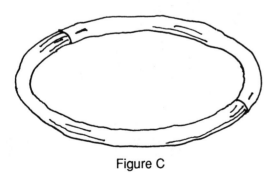

Figure C

Procedure

1. Cut all the way up one side of the bag and cut off the bottom (Fig. A).

2. Open bag and lay it flat.

3. Begin rolling the bag tightly lengthwise (Fig. B). Continue rolling to the end or trim the bag when the band becomes thick enough.

4. Staple the band together to fit your head (Fig. C).

5. Decorate as desired.

Variations

Cut the leaf pattern on page 93 out of green construction paper and fold on the dotted lines. Glue to the band for Caesar's crown (Fig. D). Add paper flowers for a Hawaiian look (Fig. E).

Figure D

Figure E

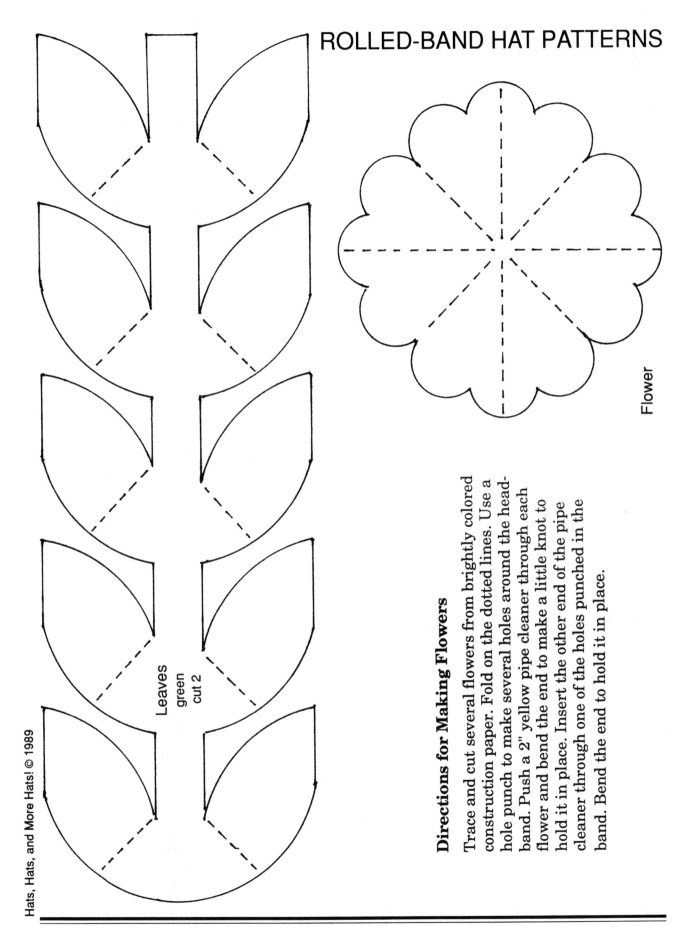

ROLLED-BAND HAT PATTERNS

Leaves
green
cut 2

Flower

Directions for Making Flowers

Trace and cut several flowers from brightly colored construction paper. Fold on the dotted lines. Use a hole punch to make several holes around the head-band. Push a 2" yellow pipe cleaner through each flower and bend the end to make a little knot to hold it in place. Insert the other end of the pipe cleaner through one of the holes punched in the band. Bend the end to hold it in place.

BERRY BASKET HAT

Materials

plastic berry basket

two 18" pieces of yarn

Procedure

1. Tie a piece of yarn to the top rim on opposite sides of the basket.

2. Invert the basket and tie the yarn under your chin (Fig. A).

Variation

Try weaving 1/2" strips of colored construction paper through the sides of the basket.

Figure A

FOIL PAN HAT

Materials

foil pie pan

36" piece of yarn

several 6" pieces of yarn

tape

hole punch

scissors

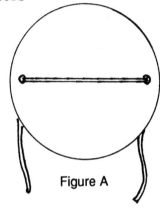

Figure A

Procedure

1. Punch a hole on two opposite sides of the pan near the rim.

2. Invert the pan and thread a 36" piece of yarn across the pan and thread it down through the holes (Fig. A). Tape the yarn in place.

3. Punch holes around the rim of the pie pan about 1" apart.

4. Fold a 6" piece of yarn in half. Thread the folded end through a hole on the pie pan and pull the free ends through the loop (Fig. B). Repeat with each hole.

5. Decorate as desired.

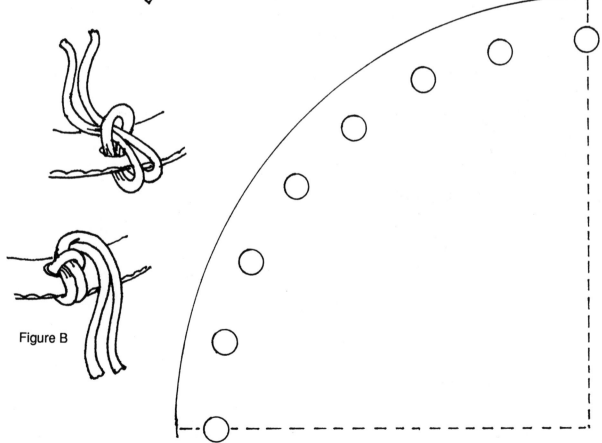

Figure B

Hats, Hats, and More Hats! © 1989

CAP

Materials

24" square of fabric

36" piece of narrow fabric ribbon

scissors

pencil

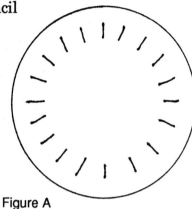

Figure A

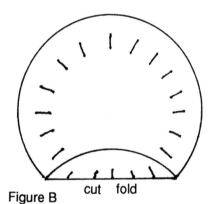

cut   fold

Figure B

Figure C

Procedure

1. Round the edges of the 24" square to make a circle.

2. Use the pencil to draw small lines on the fabric to indicate where to cut small slits around the edge of the circle about 4" from the edge (Fig. A).

3. Pinch the fabric to make a fold where there is a pencil line and cut through the fold with scissors to make a slit (Fig. B).

4. Thread the ribbon through the slits (Fig. C).

5. Place the fabric on your head and pull on the ends of the ribbon until cap fits snugly.

6. Tie the ribbon in a bow.